KING OF THE SOUTH

Derell Williams

General Information

King Of The South
By: Derell Williams

All Rights Reserved. No part of this publication may be reproduced, stored in a retrieval system, or transmitted, in any form or any means – by electronic, mechanical, photocopying, recording or otherwise – without prior written permission of the "Material Owner," Derell Williams. Any such violation infringes upon the Creative and Intellectual Property of the Owner pursuant to International and Federal Copyright Law. Any queries pertaining to this "Collection" should be addressed to Publisher of Record.

Copyright © 2021: **Derell Williams**

Cover Design: ***Orange Web Graphic Design- Shelsie Myles***
Published by: ***Derell Williams***
Editor: ***Terry L. Ware, Sr.***
ISBN: ***9798746401267***

First Edition

Dedication

I want to thank God first of all. I would like to thank my beautiful wife for being in my corner for 20 plus years, my family and friends who believed in me and even the ones they didn't. Every person in my life that played a key role for me to arrive at this point in life. This is something I've been putting off for over a decade, the wait is over! Now that being said, I Introduced to you:

"*KING OF THE SOUTH*."

Table of Contents

Dedication ii
Prologue 1

Chapter 1
DODGE CITY 3

Chapter 2
ADAPTING 2 A NEW ENVIRONMENT 11

Chapter 3
KIM 23

Chapter 4
MISTER 36

Chapter 5
THE KING IS DEAD 54

Chapter 6
A VERBAL COMMITMENT 74

Chapter 7
VENGEFUL THOUGHTS 101

Chapter 8
A REAL FAMILY REUNION 117

Chapter 9
THIS MUST END NOW 136

KING OF THE SOUTH

Derell Williams

Prologue

"Muthafucka, didn't I tell you that I needed you to have my money today?" "COME ON, FRENCHY! I got half of it on me now. PLEASE STOP!!!"

"HALF! Muthafucka, did I give you half of my SHIT, BITCH? NO! I gave you all of my shit! All of my money."

"COME ON, FRENCHY! PLEASE, man, don't break my hand. I'll get the rest of your money today.

Frenchy, don't break his hand, man. THINK!" "About what? What is there to think about? I put my dope in his hand. This will be a reminder to his ass. Dope in his hand, money not in my hand, leads to a fucking broken hand."

"Frenchy, what about the garage? Who gonna fix the cars?" "You're right, Doc." "OH, MY

LEG!!! OH MY GOD, MY LEG!!!" "Now get that nigga fixed so that he can fix Doc's car."

Chapter One

DODGE CITY

My name is King, King A. Wright. At the time, I was only eight years of age. A kid shouldn't have to be a witness to some of the things I've seen, and I tell you, I've witnessed a lot at an early age, thanks to my father, who raised his kids not to ever question his decisions. My father was the ruler of the jungle, the Projects, the concert jungle. Dodge City is what we called our Projects. Frenchy, my father, did things his way. He would always say, "My way is LAW."

I was told by some of my other brothers and sisters that I didn't have a name until I was two years old. My father named me King A. Wright at my second birthday party. I was too young to remember. From my birth until the age of two, I was called Champ, Man, Sugar, and Do-It. Out of all my nicknames, the one I could remember was Do-It. As a child, I could remember my father and his friends saying Do-It (Do-It). I was one badass kid.

Marcus Wright, better known as Frenchy, was given that name by his older cousin Nick, who said that Marcus looked like one of those French painters who got paid a lot of money for his paintings. He always dressed like he had a million bucks. He even wore a Kangol tipped to the side and smoked a long wood-tip cigar like a French man.

Frenchy Blue was from Dodge City on the Westside of town. Some of the old heads from back in the day would say that Frenchy was the Mob's prodigy son. Most people look at the saying as a rumor. This one older Indian woman stayed right next to the projects in a small house with about two acres of land. This woman would come out of her house right before daybreak screaming at the top of her lungs, at the same time every morning, "Marcus Wright is the son of the DEVIL. I TELL YOU! HE IS THE SON OF THE DEVIL, I TELL YOU!" Most people paid her no mind and would say things like, "that lady is fucking crazy".

Around midday, I would stand on top of the hill of the projects and watch as this Indian woman performed her daily ritual. She would do this dance in her front door, then she would disappear within a bunch of smoke. The white smoke that flowed out of the doors and the windows of that house always seemed to flow in my direction to this very day.

For the most part, I had a pretty normal childhood. I had friends that I would play with on the backside of the hill. Red Hill is what we called it. Red Hill was on the backside of the Projects that we played on as kids. It was a very dangerous, rocky-like hill which had the looks of a small mountain. The only time we got the chance to play on Red Hill was when our parents were drunk or throwing a party, which was every day of the week. Our parents didn't approve of us playing there. Red Hill caused an average of at least fifty to sixty broken bones yearly. I broke my leg twice and my arm once. But that was nothing because all of my friends had me beat. My best friend Mister held the record for the most broken bones, which was seven.

We would use the Red Hill as a part of our initiation throughout the years. We would trick all of the new kids who moved in the hood or just visited someone who lived in the hood to slide down Red Hill riding a cardboard box more than once. If they didn't break something on their body on the first time down Red Hill, the second time would get them. It was only right to let Mister get all of the street credit for someone's child laying at the bottom of Red Hill, with some part of their bone sticking out of their skin. Half of the Projects would be on hand to watch a crew of firemen and paramedics try their best to put them back together. We had a name for those fools; we called them Humpty Dumpties.

Every time I stood there watching a broken-up kid, I would go into this daydream about that book about the egg that fell off the wall. I would come up with these 'blueprints of badness' just to let my friends take the credit. It was okay cause I never got in trouble for my bad ideas, all-cause my friends was willing to take all the credit.

On my tenth birthday, I didn't receive any gifts from anyone, so I asked my mama why didn't I get any gifts for my birthday. She said, 'go ask your father,' knowing I wouldn't ask him all the time. I didn't ask my father because everyone knew that his word was always LAW! My father called me to come into the room, where he was sitting at the foot of his king-sized bed that looked like it belonged in a palace. I walked into the darkroom, filled with smoke that I could see because of the TV's light.

"Come in, son," his voice called out to me as I approached to sit on the floor at the foot of his bed, as I always did. My father and I had this bond. It was strange. It was like we could read each other's minds for about a minute. We had this understanding without ever discussing the situation. Usually, when I was called to his room, he would be watching some type of mob film. I would walk in, sit on the floor and begin to watch whatever he was watching. As we watched the film, we never said a word to each other until the movie ended. Then that's where the conversation would begin.

"You're ten now, right?" "Yes sir, Pops." "Kool; Kool, and I bet you want to know why we didn't get you any presents." "Yes sir." "Okay then, I will tell you cause I feel that you are ready." "King, my son, you are mature for your age, and I know there is a lot of question you would like to ask me, right?" "Right!" "Okay then, my gift to you for your tenth birthday is all of the knowledge I have. I will give it to you. Go head sport, shoot. But before you start, let me answer the number one question that's been on your mind ever since you was three or four years old. The reason it took me the first two years of your life to name you was because I was told by my great grandmother that you would come." "What do you mean Pops, about

I would come?" "Stand up, son. Look in the mirror and tell me what you see." "I see me, Pops." He stood up, walked up to the mirror, stood behind me, and asked me again. "Now, what do you see?" "I see me. I see you standing behind me."

He took out his cigar, lit it, and blew a small cloud of smoke into the mirror. As the smoke disappeared, all I could see in that mirror was me. As I looked over my shoulder, my father was still standing there, but I could no longer see him in the mirror. As I stared into the mirror, another cloud of smoke cloaked the mirror for the second time. When the smoke cleared, all I could see in the mirror was my father, who looked like a bigger version of myself.

He asks me once again, "Now what do you see, son?" "I see, I see me, Pops. I'm a grown man, Pops. How could it be? I'm only ten."

Chapter Two

ADAPTING 2 A NEW ENVIRONMENT

"Good morning, Ms. Ann, can Kim come out and play today?" "Not now, she got chores to do. Plus, she still in the bed sleeping, where you should be, boy. It's six o'clock in the morning, and Lord knows a child your age should be in bed as well. "I'm always up at daybreak, Ms. Ann." "And why is that son?" "I don't sleep well at night, Ms. Ann." "I told Lucy she needed to get you some help or send you to church with me on Sunday so that God could lay his healing hands on you. PRAISE JESUS, HALLELUJAH!"

I hated her wanna be sanctified ass. Always up in other people's business, with her messy ass. Always talking about people behind their backs, but still smiling in their faces.

"OK, Ms. Ann, I will talk to you later. I'll tell my auntie what you said about the church thing." "OK, baby, tell Lucy that I'm having one of my bible study groups on Saturday night at seven o'clock." "I will, Ms. Ann."

The Good Lord knows that if I told my auntie anything that she said for the fifth time, she would start cursing like hell. If she only knew some of the stories that my Aunt Lucy had told me about her. When I first came to live with my aunt, she would talk for hours at a time about this neighborhood, and the people that lived in it, where to go, and who to hang out with. But my dad always told me not to believe everything that I heard and half of the shit you might think you saw. Plus, my dad told me that ninety percent of people would lie to you in a heartbeat so that they can stay two or three steps ahead of you in the game of life.

When I was a few years younger, it sounded like my dad was mad at the world. But as I got a little older, I came to understand his point of view on life and the people I would encounter in my short time here on this earth. Many evil people on this earth were always doing anything to make a dollar.

"HA KING!!!" COME OVER HERE, LIL CUZ!!!"

I didn't recognize that voice, but at the time, my focus was on the sidewalk, making sure that I didn't step on any cracks. It was an old superstition that was rooted in the Deep South. While walking, if you stepped on a crack, something terrible would happen, and your mama would break her back. I loved my mama and didn't want to see anything happen to her.

"KING!"

There was that voice again, so I stopped walking and looked up in the direction that the voice came from. It was my cousin, Jay. Jay was my Auntie Lucy's only son. Jay was at the corner of 4th and 5th Street, hanging out with his crew like he did every Saturday morning.

"Wassup Jay?" I asked as I was crossing the street. "Where are you coming from, cuz? Don't tell me you are coming from Ann's house to check for Kim?" He said with a big smile on his face." It's cool cuz, all the youngsters in the neighborhood be checking for little Kim, she a cutie, but anyway cuz, I want you to hang out with me later on today if that's cool with you?" "Yeah, that's cool Jay." "OK, it's a bet lil' cuz. Pick you up from the house around five or six o'clock den." "OK, den Jay, Cool."

Jay was one of my favorite cousins who I looked up to. I had to look up to him, he stood about six-feet-four-inches tall and weighed about 225 pounds. His skin was black as coal and looked like silk. His body looked like he worked out a lot, but he never did. His eyes were fiery red, like the mad bulls you would see on T.V. He was a male version of my Granny, and she didn't play the radio, no channels at all. Jay had that bad attitude just like her.

Jay was what people would call a real lady's man. The women loved him. When I first came to town, he took me riding with him, and we stopped at the store to gas up his ride. I stayed in the car while Jay went to pay for the gas. A candy red

Chevy Blazer pulled up a few pumps down from where we were parked. This woman got out of the truck and started walking toward the store. At least we thought she was a woman. I tell you, this girl looked like an ebony queen. I mean, straight out of the Jet Magazine Beauty of the Week.

As soon as Jay approached her, and he started talking to her, I heard a voice yell out, "YOU CAN'T TALK TO HER!" So Jay turned in the direction of the red truck and said, "WHY NOT!!!" As the woman got out of the red truck and started walking towards Jay, she said, "That's my daughter, she's only fourteen."

Jay and I were both shocked! As Jay responded, "Fourteen?" This woman looked mad as hell! "YES! Fourteen!" She replied. But that didn't faze Jay; he was a real player, a smooth talker. "Your daughter!" "YES, MY DAUGHTER," the woman said with an attitude. "Damn, mama, you're lying to me, you sure you aren't sisters?" The lady smiled and said, "No, that's my daughter!" "Damn, mama, you look familiar, what's your name?" "Why you want to know my name when you were just trying to talk to my daughter?" "NO, mama, it wasn't like that, she just looked like this girl that I went to school with, so I was gonna ask her what her name was." "So what year did you graduate, Mom?" " In '74." "Girl, I graduated in '75. did you go to North Charleston High?" "YES, I did!" "GIRL, I knew I knew you. What you said your name was?'

"My name is Lisa." "Lisa, dat's right. Girl, I was crazy about you." "And what's your name?" "My name is Jay, but my friends call me Jay Rock. You can call me Jay Rock, friend." "I don't remember you, Jay Rock." "I know, I wasn't as popular as you, and I was a grade under you, as well, but I had the biggest crush on you girl!" Crush! Stop playing!" "GIRL I'm not playing. I was a boy then, but I'm all man now!" "I can see dat, Jay Rock, you are all man!" "OK Lisa, nice talking to you, I gotta go, I have somewhere to be and I don't want be late."

As Jay started to turn around, the lady called him back, grabbed his hand, and started writing something in his hand. When Jay got back to the car, I asked him what she said and what she wrote in his hand. He started laughing as he began telling me about the conversation he had with the lady. After listing to what Jay had told me, I began to understand what he was trying to teach me about getting women's attention.

He would say the key to getting her attention was using a distraction. The biggest distraction was the more she would start to pay attention to what you were saying to her. He also explained why most guys took their hard-earned money and went to buy cars, jewelry, and clothes. He said it's all just one big distraction to get a woman's attention. Jay was a real player when it came to the ladies. He never lost when it came to women. He didn't need what most of the guys were using to get a woman's attention. In his conversation with women, all he did was hit close to home, which was the biggest distraction ever in a woman's eyes. They say home is where the heart is, and man, that was a true statement if I ever heard one.

My cousin Jay was a player in more than one way. The boy had all kinds of talent. The boy could round ball his ass off; he had a full basketball scholarship to South Carolina University when he was in high school. Jay played shooting guard, and everyone that found out that he was my cousin tends to tell me that Jay would have made it to the National Basketball Association if his attitude wasn't so bad. In his freshman year in college, he got into a fight with two of his teammates at practice and ended up putting both the guys in the hospital. I was told that the first guy he hit was knocked out cold with one punch, and the other had to have some emergency surgery to save his left eye. Jay knocked the kid's eye out the socket. He messed those boys up badly.

The President of the University wanted to have a winning program so bad that he only gave Jay a slap on the wrist, which was probation for only one week, but he couldn't make it through that. Two days later, Jay started a small riot in the lunchroom cafeteria. The University had no choice but to take Jay's scholarship from him and banned him from the college campus for five years. That didn't stop Jay from going back to the University as he pleased.

"Auntie Lucy, I'm back!" "Boy, where you been?" "Outside talking to Jay." "Don't lie to me, King, you left this house around six o'clock this morning. Heading where is what I would like to know. OK, King spit it out now!"

I wasn't lying to my Auntie Lucy. I just left out the part about going to see Kim at Ms. Ann's house because I didn't want to hear her talk about that lady this early in the morning. I wasn't a liar, my Mom used to tell me one thing I should always do, and another thing I should never do was always to speak my mind and never lie unless I was facing a lot of time in prison or someone had a gun to my head.

"King, I'm still waiting on you to answer me!" "I went to see could Kim come out and play with me today." "Kim huh? So, what did Ann say to you about coming to her house at six o'clock in the morning?" "Just dat Kim was still in bed and had chores to do when she got up." "Was dat all she said, King?" "No ma'am, she also said that she wanted you to come to her bible study group on Saturday night at seven o'clock. Plus, she wanted you to let her take me to church with her as well." "NO WAY! No way in hell dat I would let you go to church with her hypocritical ass! And I wouldn't be caught dead at one of her fake ass bible study groups again, which afterwards will turn to anything goes when the good book had been put away. Forgive me King, I don't like talking bad about people, but they ain't right son, playing with God like dat." "I understand, Auntie." "Listen to me son, if you decided dat you want go and praise the Lord, just let me know and I will take you myself. OK!" "OK, auntie." "So, we do have dat understanding, right nephew?" "Yes ma'am!" "OK, den King, go wash your hands so you can eat." "OK, auntie."

After eating breakfast, I went straight to my room. All I could think about was getting up with Jay that evening. Man, I knew we were gonna have a ball.

Chapter Three

KIM

"Kim! Kim! Get your butt out of that bed!!! Did you hear me, girl?" "I heard you, mama, sheesh!" "What you say under your breath, lil girl!" "I didn't say anything, mama." "Stop lying and get your tail up and come wash these dishes." "Ok, Mom, let me wash my face and brush my teeth first." "Hurry up so that I can cook for my bible study group tonight!"

I'm so tired of her and her holy friends every Saturday night! Bible studies, my butt! More like club night at Ann's house, ughhh!!! She makes me so mad at times like I work for her and her friends.

"What took you so long, Kim?" "I had to clean up myself first mama before I could clean up the house." "Oh, you think that's funny with your smart tail?" "No ma'am." "What did I tell you about trying to be a smart aleck?" "I'm not mama, I'm just saying." "What are you saying, Kim?" "Nothing mama." "I know nothing, Kim. You are fourteen now and in a couple of years, you will be off to college." "I know mama." "Well, do you know that you will have to clean up after yourself, Ms. Know-It-All." "Yes ma'am." "Well, I will tell you, like my Mother used to tell me, practice makes perfect. The more you do things, the more it will become routine. Don't forget to sweep and mop the floor as well." "I'll be back, I'm going to the store to get the rest of the things I'll need for my party."

Party is right! I thought it was a bible study group. She needs to stop! Every Saturday, it's the same old song, waking me up at seven o'clock talking about clean up, going to college, and what her Mother used to tell her. She loved trying to pretend like I wasn't a very organized person so that she could have me cleaning up her and her friends' junk. My room was always very clean and organized. I had all of my ball shoes, JV uniforms, and sports gear in my closet, and all of my girly clothing in my drawers, which was where they stayed all the time. I'm a ballplayer; I had no need to wear dresses, make-up, or tight jeans.

Ring… Ring… Ring…

I wonder which one of her friends is calling now? "HELLO!" "Kim, what are you doing girl?" "Cleaning up girl." "That's right, it's Saturday, Ms. Ann getting ready for one of her HOE downs, and I'm not talking about the Wild-Wild Western!" "Sue, don't be talking about my Mother like that."

"Come on girl, you know I'm just playing, you know I love Ms. Ann and will kick anyone's ass if they say anything bad about her." "I know you will Sue. I just will be so happy when I leave and go off to college." "I know girl! It's not far though, Ms. Ann likes to use you as a maid on Saturday." "Don't forget that we are in church all throughout the day on Sunday as well." "Man, that's gotta suck feet. Girl, you really don't have a weekend to yourself. I wouldn't want to be your blood sister, Cinderella," she laughed.

"Not funny, evil stepsister!" "So, what I do?" "That's my point; you never do anything to help me out of this hellhole." "That's your Mom, not mine, and girl you know I don't mind coming over there to help you clean up but waiting on those friends of your mama's hand and foot, not my style." "I know right, I wouldn't wish this on my worst enemy. School all week, then dis on the weekend. Lord, please save me!"

"Girl, why don't you call Jay? Didn't you say that he's the reason that you have all of them different scholarships. Plus, you know your mamma really likes him." "See! Girl, sometimes I wish I didn't tell you things." "Then who would you tell them to? I'm your best friend, and all I'm doing is looking out for your best interest."

She was right! Sueann was my best friend, and she had been looking out for me ever since we were in the 3rd grade. When this girl named Josette used to bully me by taking all of my crayons and put glue in my hair, Sue came to my rescue by pushing Josette over a lego block castle. Ever since that day, we were inseparable. I loved Sue, and I wished she could leave with me when I went off to college, but I knew it would somewhat be impossible now that she had a two-month-old baby.

Sue started dating this guy in middle school named Rob. *Rob, Rob the Heartthrob* is what all the girls in school called him. Rob was a grade ahead of us and had a lot of different girls. He was a real playboy, which was the name of the crew he ran with. The Playboys had all the prettiest girls in the school. Plus, Rob and his brothers throw the best house parties. I guess you can say they were the fraternity of our high school. "Sue, I'll hit you back in a few minutes; I got to make another call." "Go head girl! It's about time for me to feed Robert, Jr. Talk with you later." "Ok, talk with you in a little bit."

"Kimberly!!! I'm back!!" Good thing I got a chance to make my phone call before she got home cause Lord knows she was like the FBI when it came down to anything that went on in this house! "Kimberly, get out here and help me get these groceries out of the car." "I'm coming, mama." "I'm waiting, Kim. Ok, about time you show up, go get those bags out of the car for your Mother." "Ok, mama, what are you cooking?" "Well Kim, I'm cooking some meatloaf, mac & cheese, green beans, fried chicken, mash potatoes, and fried okra."

Every Saturday, my Mother had the same routine, going all out of her way just to try to impress her friends and some of the members of her church. She needs to stop. "Kimberly, I'm about to go take a bath, so I need you to listen out for Shirley. She's coming over to help me prepare the food for my bible study tonight. Ok, Kimberly." "I hear you mama, sheesh." "What you say under your breath, little girl?" "I said, yes mama!"

Damn, sometimes I think this whole house is bugged. I gotta get out of this place, just for a day or so. I'm starting to talk to myself more than normal, and if I stay in this house one more Saturday, I just might start to answer myself back. Lord knows I can't let that happen to me.

RING…RING…RING…RING…

"I'M COMING! Hold your horses!" I'm talking on the telephone now. Someone, please save me from this madness. "HELLO!!! HELLO!!!" "Dang Short Stuff, calm down. It's me." "JAY?" "Yes, it's me. Are you ready?" "So ready! Jay, where are we going, and what are we doing today?" "Come on, Short Stuff, you know what we're doing; it will never change." "Practice, right?" "That's right, practice. Cause if I couldn't make it due to my bad attitude, I know it will be different with you cause you are a real sweetheart." "So what time are you coming?" "I will be there around 10:00." "Ok, I'll be waiting!" "Ok, see you den, Short Stuff. Bye-bye!" "Bye!"

Jay has been calling me Short Stuff for as long as I could remember. But, compared to all of my friends and classmates, I stand over them like a tree. I'm fourteen years old and six-and-a-half feet tall. I've always been tall for my age, which was hard to deal with when I was a child. Kids made a lot of jokes about my height throughout the years, but thanks to Jay, those days are behind me. Being a lot taller than normal had me self-conscious for years until one day I was walking home from school crying, and as I passed by Jay, who was outside sitting on the porch. He called me over with a concerned look on his face and asked, "What's the matter, Kim?"

At first, I just looked up at him and tried to wipe away the tears. He knew by just looking at me that this had been going on for a long time now. "Kim, sweetheart, what's the matter? You can tell me." I knew Jay because his Mom and my Mom were very good friends at the time. But looking at them now, you would've thought they were enemies for years. Jay was always very nice to me when my Mother and I would come over to visit his Mom, so I decided to tell him what I had been going through for years. As I started to explain what I was going through, all he did was look at me and listen.

As soon as I stop talking, he smiled and said, "Stand next to me." At first, I was trying to understand what he was trying to do. So, I decided to stand next to Jay, who stood about six-feet-two-inches tall. He looked like a giant over me.

He then said, "You ain't that tall, Kim, the people around you are just shorter than you are." Then he explained how being taller has its advantages. As I started to leave, Jay called out to me, I turned around to see his pretty smile. He said, "See you tomorrow, Short Stuff." That was the first day that he called me by that name.

Throughout the years, Jay had always been there for me, teaching me that being taller than others would play a big role in life. Every day after school, I would meet up with Jay at the blacktop, which was located behind his high school gym. Jay taught me the game of basketball, so he's the main reason for my success at the JV level at my High School and nationwide. Jay showed me everything that he knew about basketball. Thanks to him, I'm the number one high school player in the county, and I'm only a freshman.

I'd also received full scholarships from all of the top basketball programs in the nation. Plus, there had been people from other countries trying to sign me up for the pro level straight out of High School. But my Mom had been telling all of them that I was going to college so that I could get a free education first. Which I would happen to agree with, for once in my life. I was only fourteen, and by the time I was sixteen, I needed to be focused on college instead of what color I'd like my window drapes to be in my new house. Having a lot of money was ok, I guess, but my dad told me getting a good education would last a lifetime; money comes and goes. That's the motto that I was sticking to. Plus, financially, my family was pretty well off, thanks to my dad.

My dad worked for this Fortune 500 company that worked side-by-side with the New York Stock Exchange. He and my Mom had been divorced ever since I was five years old. A few years back, I decided to ask my Mom why her and daddy got a divorce, and she would say things like, *"you are too young to understand. but when you're older, I'll sit you down and explain them to you, but now isn't the right time."* I was only ten at the time and was trying my best to get them back together so that we could be one happy family.

That didn't work out at all. Every summer, I'd go and live with my father for a month at the end of the school year. It has been that way for as long as I could remember. My father and I didn't do a lot due to his busy work schedule. He's always on the phone making business deals which I had gotten used to throughout the years. I knew my daddy loved me because he told me all the time how beautiful I was, and without me being in his life, his world would be empty. I still hadn't figured out that last part of the quote, but I was good either way, as long as he's happy, I'd continue to pretend that I was.

Every Sunday, we went out to one of those Five-Star restaurants, where he normally asked me about the usual things, like school, sports, and boys. Afterward, he'd take me shopping for the entire next school term, which took about twelve hours. I'm not complaining because I loved when we went to Footlocker. That was a little piece of heaven for me; a girl needed her kicks for that hardwood. When we finally returned home, we'd have movie night which he always fell asleep within the first five minutes of the movie. I didn't mind because it seemed to be the only time that he got a chance to get some good rest. So, I always got a blanket, covered him up, kissed his forehead, and told him goodnight.

Chapter Four

MISTER

Twenty-one hours and thirteen minutes and I'd be out of this pissy-smelling rathole. Ninety-eight days was a long time to be off the street for a G like me. Couldn't get no real money in here, with all of these snitches and bitch-made niggas trying to tell on their mamas just to get some time cut off their sentences, pussy muthafuckas. These niggas hated to go to jail for the shit they decided to do. Muthafucka do the crime, but when their asses got caught, they couldn't do the time.

Like this pussy muthafucka Leon. When his ass was out on the streets balling, buying the bar out at the clubs, and having these dumb ass contests in the clubs called money fights, it was all good then. As soon as the Feds jammed his bitch ass with eighty pounds of marijuana, his ass took the Feds right back to the people that he got the shit from. Stupid muthafucka never did any time, didn't know shit about the law. This fool thought that his ass wasn't going to do any time. They tricked his ass and gave that nigga two years.

I couldn't believe some of these muthafuckas out here, committing all kinds of crimes and having no idea of how much time that crime carried if they were caught. After this muthafucka, Leon, told on his family's connect, it put his brothers and cousins back in poverty. If he would've kept his mouth shut, he would've only done three years. I knew I should've robbed that muthafucka Leon when I had a chance, but the only reason I didn't, was because I had a baby by his first cousin. If it wasn't for that, I would've been put that pussy muthafucka in the trunk!

"COUNT TIME!!" Man, I'm tired of this shit, with these weak ass CO's. "I SAID COUNT TIME!!!!! ALL YOU MUTHAFUCKING BASTARDS ON YOUR RACKS, NOW!"

I hated that bitch ass nigga. Thought he was tough because he had a badge. If you caught that muthafucka on the streets, he'd try to be your best friend. If I ever saw his ass out on the streets, I was going to slap his ass on GP. That nigga was the reason I'm in lockdown now, trying to put his fucking hands on me while I was trying to use the phone. As soon as he grabbed me, I turned around and pushed his weak ass in the face. You should've seen that nigga call for backup. The muthafuckas roughed me up just a little, but it wasn't shit to a gangsta though. I had been in S.E.G. for a whole month, but it was over now! I'd be home soon, and muthafuckas better pay up because the streets owed me. I'd been gone too long.

"Damn, King, you're out of jail now; it's a blessing to be free on your eighteenth birthday. Plus, you haven't been home to see your family in years. Seven years, to be exact." "I did talk to my Mom's a few times throughout the years, Aunt Lucy. My mama knows that I love her and always will. When she sent me away to Carolina, I was mad for a few years, but at that age, I couldn't understand." I'd gotten a little older, so now, when I looked back on it, I tried to convince myself it was for the best. I hadn't seen my mama since I was eleven. Guess it won't hurt anything if I hit the road and got some fresh air. Alabama, here I come!

Thirty miles out? DAMN, this was a long ass ride, but I was here now, so I guessed I would make one more stop at this intersection right off of Freeway Exit 21 before I hit the city limits. Man, I wasn't sure what kind of cigars to get. I didn't think they sold the wraps that I normally bought this deep in the south.

"Can I help you, Sir? SIR!" "Are you talking to me, sweetheart?" "Yes, I am. So now, can I help you?!" "Damn ma, calm down. It's a true saying, Rome wasn't built in a day," I laughed. "Man, you ain't in no damn Rome, dis is Alabama, and you are holding up my line!" Damn, I thought people were rude up North. I see the southern hospitality went out the door with this lady, I thought with a chuckle. "I'm sorry, Miss, let me fill up on pump three and buy this Country Time Lemonade."

"Hey, Mister!!!" "Wut dat Teto?" "Buddy down Red Hill said that GG had robbed him earlier." "GG DID WHAT!!! And who the fuck is Buddy?" "Sorry, Mister, you know the dude name Mike that be buying two or three-quarters of hard a day." "Yeah, I know, Mike, he shops with a few of my cousins; he don't shop with me. And you said that GG robbed him earlier?" "Yep, but not with a gun; he finessed him with the UnReal you gave him." "Oh, he did, did he?" I couldn't help but laugh. "Go down Red Hill and tell Mike I'm gonna look out for him on what he lost fuckin with GG." "Ok, be right back with him."

GG was always thinking too fucking small, and that's the reason his ass never could keep a dollar. I bet couldn't nobody find this nigga. UnReal was something I cooked up in the kitchen after I fucked off a good bit of cash. It's made out of candle wax, white flour, water, and grease. The candlewax was melted down in a pot on the stove. Then, you added the other three ingredients: the white flour, water, then the grease, just to give it that oily look. Once all four were combined, I then took it out of the pot, shaped it as I saw fit, then placed it in the freezer for about twenty minutes, so it could harden up. After the twenty minutes was up, it was like magic, something that looked like crack rock that wasn't crack rock; therefore, we named it UnReal. I said all of that just to say, UnReal is fake crack.

"Hey, Mister!!!" "Wassup, Teto?" "I got Mike with me; open the door!" What Mike didn't know was that I was the king of finessing niggas. I put niggas down on this hustle, and since he never shopped with me, you knew I had to hook him up.

Seven years later, my Mom's still lived in the projects. That was one thing I would never understand due to her sending me off to stay with my Aunt Lucy in Charleston, South Carolina. When I was a little younger, my Aunt Lucy would try her best to try and make me understand the reason my mama sent me off to stay with her, saying things like, *"your mama wanted a better life for you."* Some better life! I was facing some serious time in prison for trying to purchase three guns, an AR-15, a Glock 40 with an extended fifty-round clip, and a 223 semi-automatic, from this guy named Rob who turned out to be an informant for the DEA of Charleston. The rumor floating around the county jail in Charleston was that Rob sold this sixteen-year-old kid from the suburbs a handgun, which the kid's parents found in his room. They called the cops to scare their son straight. I know this sounded cliché, but yes, it's the same story. The cops told the kid if he didn't tell them where he got the gun from, they were gonna take him to jail for a very long time. Couldn't be mad at the kid for saving his own tail. I was almost certain that this kid with the silver spoon lifestyle had a brighter future than Rob or me.

While sitting in that cell for the last few months, all I could think about was making sure that this muthafucka Rob didn't come to the arraignment, so I could have my lawyers ask that the judge to throw the case out. Some people really have no business being in the game, I thought, shaking my damn head. Muthafuckas didn't respect the rules of the game, and Rob's dumb ass should've known better than to be selling guns to some damn suburb kids! This clown ass nigga was overcharging the rich kids just to make a couple of extra hundred dollars but overlooked the rules of the game. All money ain't good money: Rule #10 in the Hustler's Handbook.

I'd finally made it. I saw this place hadn't changed much! "YO HOMIE!!!" I heard someone yell as I stepped out of my car. "WHO YOU WITH!" That was slang or short for who are you looking for. Since I was obviously by myself, I knew these guys were with the shit. So, I grabbed my gun and stepped out of the car.

"HEY, DUDE!! I KNOW YOU HEAR ME!" "YEAH, I HEARD YOU!!! I ain't looking for you; that's why I didn't answer you back!" "WHO THE FUCK ARE YOU TALKING TO LIKE THAT, NIGGA!!!" I didn't say another word; all I was thinking was, if these three niggas think that they are going to jump me, they are sadly mistaken.

Mister! "Wassup Mike?" "Nothing, Mister, I'm still singing the same song. Trying to make a dollar out of fifteen cents, a dime, and a nickel. But on the real, I wanted you to know that this guy sold me some bad product early dis mornin'. I don't know his name, but I have seen him around you a couple of times." "So you saying that to say what, Mike?" "It ain't nothing against you, Mister. Do you have any to sell?"

One thing I really, really didn't like was niggas confronting me when they knew who the real gangster was. I considered myself to be a pretty fair guy at times; it all depended on the situation. I had done a lot of off-the-wall shit, but that was just me.

"Yeah, Mike, wut you need?" "I need a half of an ounce, if you got it, Mister." "I got it, wait here while I go weigh it up."

This muthafucka Mike didn't know me for being a finesser, but he did know that I would rob a muthafucka in a heartbeat. he was probably in the other room sweating bullets while thinking about bullets literally.

"MIKE!" "Yeah, Mister." "Come in the back." "Ok, on the way." "Here you go, fourteen grams and an extra three grams to help you with the loss from earlier." "Ok, thanks, Mister. What I owe for the half?" "Five-hundred and fifty dollars." This fool pulled out the cash and handed it to me like you would a cashier in a grocery store. *POW!! POW!!!* "SOMEBODY SHOOTING, MISTER!!!" "I'm standing right here Teto, I heard it!"

Them niggas thought it was a game, talking shit, thinking they were going to whip my ass. That one nigga was lucky I didn't aim for his head. As soon as I began walking up the stairs, these guys started to come after me. So I waited until they were about seven feet up on me, and I turned around and fired two shots off.

BOOM!!!!!BOOM!!!!! "WUT'S UP NOW, NIGGAS?" The nigga I hit with the two shots started to fall to the ground, screaming and begging for his life, "MAN, DON'T KILL ME!!!! PLEASE DON'T KILL ME!!!!"

I was more focused in these situations and didn't panic because someone could get killed, and it wouldn't be me. I was so focused that everything around was moving in slow motion, like in a movie. No movies here; I just had to keep my wits about the situation so that I could plan my escape. As the guy hit the ground, I stood over him as his other two partners ran off and left him to die. I started to give him a few more hot ones to finish him off, but everything was back at real speed now. People started coming outside, looking and pointing their fingers in my direction; that's when I realized that this might've been the shortest visit ever. In these types of situations, you couldn't panic, so I started to run to my car. As I drove off, I didn't speed off, knowing that would've been a straight giveaway for the police. While I drive at normal speed, I happened to have driven past a total of five speeding cop cars, two fire trucks, and an ambulance. Once I noticed I was in the clear, I jumped back on 85 North, heading towards Atlanta, Georgia.

"DAMN MAINE, WHO SHOT YOU?" "I don't know, Mister. Some nigga I never seen before!" "E!! WHO SHOT MAINE?" "All I know, Mister, is dat the nigga had to be from out of town!" "Why you say dat E?" "Because the nigga had an out-of-town tag on dis black-on-black charger he was driving." "DAMN NIGGA! Wut did the tag say!!!" "South Carolina, I think!" "MISTER!!! COME OVER HERE, I HAVE TO TELL YOU SOMETHING!!!" "Ok, Ms. Wright!" "HURRY UP BOY, BEFORE THE COPS GET HERE!!!" "Yes ma'am." "Mister, I think that was my son that shot Maine." "Who, King?" "Yes, King!" "Why didn't you tell me he was coming home?" "I wanted to surprise you. Plus, spend a little time with my boy before you two got together and started catching up where y'all friendship left off. Let me call him. That boy is probably on his way back to South Carolina."

Dammit, man, that was a waste of a trip; back to South Carolina, I go!

King

RING…RING…RING…

"Who could this be? HELLO!" I answered my phone. "Boy, where are you?" "Oooh. HEY Mama!" "King, don't hey mama me, and why didn't you tell me you were coming to town?" "I was planning on surprising you." "Boy, you know it was not gonna be no darn surprise. Your Aunt Lucy called me as soon as she knew you were coming this way. You know my sister tells me everything. Are you driving a black-on-black Dodge Charger?" "Yes, I am." "How far are you out?" "I'm coming up on the Auburn exit." "Well, turn around and come on back home." "What about the cops and their niggas, mama!" "Don't worry about the guys; I know them personally, and we will take care of the cops before you arrive." "We! Who is we Mom?" "Me and Mister." "You and Mister, huh?" "Yes! See you soon, gotta go!"

Mister

That damn King took after his Pops, I thought, laughing. My man is a real gangster; I can't wait to see him again. "E!" "Wassup, Mister?" "So tell me what happened. give me the short version; we don't have much time before the MPD shows up."

The MPD is short for the Montgomery Police Department. Looked like the apple didn't fall far from the tree. If King was anything like his Pops, he didn't start shit, but he always finished it. "SPIT IT OUT, E!!!" "Well... Well..." "STOP STUTTERING NIGGA, COME ON OUT WITH IT!" "Well... You know how cousin be thinking he runs the projects when you are nowhere around?" "Ok, E, I will take it from here. So, remember, you haven't seen shit, you don't know who shot Maine, or what the guy looked like or where he came from, and go tell Mike wut I said, because dat nigga can't hold water. I know he can't wait to spread it like he was in the middle of the action when we know dat coward always the first one to run." "Ok, Mister, whatever you say."

"Calm down, Maine, you gonna live. Looks like the shot went straight through. It's not bleeding too bad. That is how you can tell that the bullet didn't hit an artery." "ARE YOU SURE I'M GONNA LIVE, MS. WRIGHT?" "Yeah, I'm sure, Maine." "WELL MS. WRIGHT, IT HURTS LIKE HELL!" "I know it burns like hell, Maine, but I need you to calm down and listen. I need you to not tell the cops anything." "WUT!!! WHY NOT!!!" "Because that was my SON!" "YOUR SON!" "YES, MY SON!" "BUT!!!BUT!!! I KNOW ALL OF YOUR KIDS! AND THE NIGGA DAT SHOT ME AIN'T ONE OF THEM!"

"MAINE, DO WUT SHE TOLD YOU!" "WUT YOU MEAN, MISTER? DID YOU HEAR WHAT SHE SAID?" "I know wut she said, and believe it!" "Ok, I see y'all ain't pulling my leg. I only have one good one left," he said, trying to make a joke. That damn Maine. No matter what we'd been through in our lives, good or bad, he would find a way to make us laugh. This crazy-ass fool, I couldn't help but laugh.

"STAND BACK!!! STAND BACK!!!" one of the medics yelled as he made his way through the crowd. It's going to be a long day, and it's only noon. Man, Man, Man, I thought, laughing out loud, this shit only happens in the hood.

Chapter Five

THE KING IS DEAD

As I pulled back into the projects, looking for a crime scene, I noticed my Mom standing on Red Hill with about nine or ten guys standing behind her. It wasn't clear to me what was going on, so I popped the trunk of my car to get my thirty-round extendo for my Smith & Wesson Glock 40, which gave me about forty-two shots if anything popped off with these guys. As I made my way up the steps towards my Moms, she and this big guy started walking in my direction. I had no idea who this guy was with her, but this fucking guy was huge. Just taking a quick calculation as I got closer, he had to stand six-three or six-four because he made my Moms' look like a kid standing next to a grown-up.

"HEYYY BABY!!!" My Mom's shouted as they approached me with her arms out to hug me. But I kept one eye on this defensive end looking muthafucka as I embraced my Mother with a hug. "Hey, Momma." "HEY, MOMMA! Boy, you are acting like you ain't happy to see me!" "I am happy to see you, But...." "BUT WHAT? Oh," she laughed out loud. "you don't remember him?" She laughed again. "He was the smallest one out of y'all." "Wassup King?" this guy said, in a somewhat familiar voice, with aggression towards me. So, I responded with aggression. "WUSSUP!!!"

You got to understand the reason for my high aggression. About two hours ago, I had to put two shots in a guy acting like I was trespassing on his property in this very spot. So being cordial to anybody in this neighborhood the last thing on my mind. "I haven't seen you in six or seven years." "MAN, HOW DO YOU KNOW ME?" "King, it's me, MISTER!" "MAN, GET THE FUCK OUT OF HERE! MISTER? IT CAN'T BE!!!"

I took another really good look at his face again. "BOY, it is Mister. Y'all talk for a second, and den come in the house. You two will have plenty of time to get caught up later!" my Momma said loudly. "DAMN MISTER, you turned out to be one big dude!" "I KNOW, RIGHT?" Mister responded. "Man, you was the smallest out of everybody that ran with us. You gotta be on some type of super growth food," I joked, laughing out loud. "Nawl King, I just started to grow two times faster than a normal kid would every year, right after your folks sent you away.

You know what, King?" "Wut's dat, Mister?" "Well no one knew where your parents sent you, nor did your family ever talk about you. For the first few years, it was strange; it was as if you never existed." "Don't feel bad, Mister. You are not the only one they didn't tell anything. I remember the day I was sent off like it was yesterday." Just thinking back on that day brings bad memories I'm not trying to relive.

"Hey, Mister, who the fuck was dat fool I shot?" "Dat was my cousin Maine." "YOUR COUSIN!!!" "Yeah, my cousin! It's cool; I talked with Maine before the ambulance carried him off to the hospital. I been told him about pushing up on people he don't know." "Tru dat Mister! And I'm glad I was in the mindset of slowing them down instead of killing them."

"KING!!!" I heard my Momma's voice echo from around the corner, so I would have to catch up with Mister later. "I'M COMING, MOM!" "Yo, Mister, get with you in a few!" "Okay, King, how long are you planning on being here in town?" "Don't know yet, partner, but we got some catching up to do!" "Fasho King, get at me!" "BET!!!"

I'd been gone for seven years, and the place don't look like it changed a bit. As soon as I turned the corner, trying to make it to my Mom's apartment, it was like déjà vu all over again. As I watched the grown-ups in the middle of the projects, my childhood flashed before my eyes again. It was a weird feeling. I stood there reminiscing about how my friends and I used to run through the square until our parents got tired of us getting on their nerves and ran us off. Those were the days.

I thought back on RED HILL, which was across the street. There were two sides of the projects: the side that Moms stayed on, where all of the adults from both sides of the project would come to the square of the neighborhood would come to party every day all day, was called Dodge City, and the other, called OK Corral. The side where me and my crew played on the hill was RED HILL.

As I stated in chapter one, our parents disapproved of us being on The Hill at all, but they were too busy partying to notice where we were until somebody's child was seriously hurt. Back then, the grown-ups used to tell us stories about Red Hill. At the time, I thought they were making things up just to scare us off Red Hill; it turned out the stories were true. On top of Red Hill, there were three huge oak trees that branches hung over the side. Some of the stories we were told were that the slave owners would hang the slaves that would try to run away or the ones that would steal bread just so that their families wouldn't starve. Four hundred years of white folks treating blacks like they were animals, and in this day and age, it's just a new version that locks brothers up in cages and shoots them down in the streets without doing any time in jail for their actions.

To this very day, I still found it funny when I heard people say what's done in the dark will soon come to light, and what goes around will come back around. Plus, we all know karma is a bitch. Saying all of that to say that there were hundreds, maybe thousands of slaves hung off of Red Hill. So, the Federal government purchased the property and was planning on turning that side of the project into a Memorial for the slaves that were butchered and hung on Red Hill. I couldn't even imagine living back then in that era. I would've been like Nat Turner or Harriet Tubman. I knew this due to my rebellious spirit.

As I continued to walk through the square, more and more of my childhood came back to me.

At that moment, I started to realize that I had a pretty good childhood but a short window of time to enjoy it. My parents sent me away to live with my Aunt Lucy, who was a single parent with one child, my cousin Jay who was about twenty-one at the time, so I had to grow up fast.

"MOMMA!!! WHERE ARE YOU?" I yelled as I walked through the front door of my parent's apartment. "IN THE KITCHEN, BABY!" she yelled back. Walking through my parents' apartment was like walking through a small plushed-out mansion. My parents always had nice furniture and electronics throughout the apartment as far back as I could remember. My Mom's never had to work; my dad took care of everything, and everybody in the family, financially. He owned the neighborhood mechanic shop. If you're wondering where my dad is, he's at the Alabama DOC (Alabama Department of Corrections). To put it in shorter terms, he's in prison.

I didn't know all the details of why he had to go to prison. I only knew what my Aunt Lucy told me. She told me some guy owed my Pops some money for fixing his car. This guy decided that he wasn't going to pay my Pops, so my Pops and my uncle LeRoy threw the guy in the trunk of his car and brought him back to the projects. They dragged him to an empty apartment, tied him to a chair, and put a whoopin' on him badly. The guy ended up staying in the ICU at Jackson Hospital for about two weeks, but my cousin Jay told me that the guy didn't file any charges. The State of Alabama filed the charges against my Pops for Conspiracy to Kidnap, Assault in the First, and Attempted Murder.

    I haven't talked with or seen my dad in six years. I was around twelve years old the last time I had a conversation with him, a few months before he went to prison. My Father, Marcus Wright, AKA Frenchy Blue, told my Momma and the rest of his baby Mommas that he didn't want any of his kids to see him while he was away doing time. For the longest time, I was feeling some type of way about it. But now, I'm okay with the decision he made for his life.

"Hey, Momma! So what have you been doing all of these years?" "I see you haven't lost that sense of humor, King." "Now sit down so we can talk." Momma didn't look like she'd aged one day since I'd been gone. She's still as beautiful as ever, with that smile that lit up the entire room.

"So what you want to talk about?" First, she started by telling me that they loved me, they sent me away for my safety, and how it was the plan to send me off before I became a teenager where only them and my aunt Lucy knew. Then she explained how she and my dad set my Aunt Lucy up in South Carolina by buying her a house and paid her bills for thirteen years. I was waiting on my Mom's to stop and catch her breath, but I knew she hadn't even begun to crack the surface on what she was telling me. I was surprised but not shocked because

I knew deep down in my heart that my parents wouldn't have sent me away and forget about me, almost to the point where I had no interest in having any family besides Jay and Aunt Lucy. But the more and more she talked, the more some of the things I hadn't understood started to fall into place.

I could never figure out why my parents woke me up around 1:30 in the morning with one packed suitcase and put me in a car with a total stranger. Still, to this day, I have no idea who the guy was. I swear I used to see this guy throughout the years in South Carolina, but I wasn't sure until I asked her who was the guy that took me to South Carolina. She responded by saying, "His name is Todd Smith. He's your bodyguard." Guardian Angel is what she called him. "TODD!!! Would you come out here for a minute!"

My Mom's called out loudly, and I watched this guy walk into the kitchen. This guy was an average-sized man. "Hello, Mr. King." "Hi," I responded to this guy that I knew for a fact now that I had been seeing. The guy walked up to me and shook my hand. Before I could start asking him any questions, he stood back, and my Mom's took over as if she could read my mind. She said that Todd had been watching over me the entire time while I was in South Carolina. He was making sure that I could live as a normal teenager, plus keeping tabs on the people who wanted to hurt me. I had no idea why someone would want to hurt me, but I was sure that my Mom's was going to enlighten me on that.

As I continued to listen, she told me that Todd was the best at what he did. He used to work for the Secret Service under the Clinton Administration, which was shocking to me until she went on to tell me that Todd spoke five different languages English, Russian, Italian, Spanish, and Japanese. He was an ex-Marine that graduated at the top of the class in every division. He was hired on by President Clinton as a bodyguard sniper. As soon as President Clinton's eight-year term at the White House was over, he retired and went on the market as a freelance worker.

I was also told that Todd was called in by some powerful people, whom my Father did business with. These people were very dangerous, I was told, but were considered very good friends of my family. Plus, my Mom's confirmed what I was thinking, and that was that the people she was describing were Mafia. At first, I wasn't shocked, but now I was blown away and in total disbelief of most of the things I was hearing come out of my Mother's mouth.

"Hold on, Mom! So you're telling me dat this family is tied in with the MOB!" "No Son, that's not what I'm saying." "So, what you are saying?" At that Moment, I was confused. but then she came out and said, "We are the MOB, King, and you are the heir to the throne, the bloodline, and that was the main reason for sending you away and making sure that no one knew your whereabouts."

She then explained that we were at war with the southern parts of Alabama, which included Greenville, down to Mobile, Alabama. I swear this was a lot to stomach, only being seventeen and getting a bomb like this dropped at the front door like the early morning paper. I needed a Moment to absorb some of this information so that I could take in more. The way this was going, it looked like this was going to be a long night. "King! Son, are you okay?" "Yes Momma, I'm good. just give me about five minutes before you continue."

So she nodded her head as I got up from the table and started to walk through the house. I noticed the man-sized mirror was located in the same place as when I was a kid. As I approached my parents' room door, I started to reminisce about that very last conversation that my Pops and I had in there.

Right in front of that mirror, you could see from the hallway stairs as soon as you reach the second floor. Approaching the mirror, I could tell something was about to happen. I had this strange feeling come over my body, and when I heard a loud scream coming from downstairs, I turned around and started running in the direction of screams. As I got closer, the screams turned into sobs, followed by crying. As I reached the bottom of the stairwell, I saw my Mom's on the floor and Mister stooping down on one knee like he was trying to hold her up.

As tears ran down her face, I yelled out, "MOMMA, WUT'S WRONG???!!!" She then turned around with tears in her eyes flowing like the ALABAMA river then said, "HE'S DEAD BABY! HE'S DEAD! THEY KILLED YOUR FATHER!!!!" If the information that my Mom's laid on me earlier wasn't enough, now this. This couldn't be happening. This couldn't be true!

One hour later, there were about two hundred people outside standing in the square. I tell you, the word traveled fast about the passing of my Pops. People started coming from all over town and beyond to show their support, so I thought. Todd informed me that half of the people outside owed my Pops money, and the other 50% of them wanted him dead, so I was to trust no one. So it would be best for me to stay out of the way. Then Todd explained to me the art of war by saying whoever held the element of surprise would win 99% of the time, and my element of surprise was that no one knew what I looked like.

I stood off while watching my Mom's communicate with this couple. Both dressed like today was the funeral day, with these other two guys who had their bodyguards, also dressed in black. Mister stood over my Mother as if he was her bodyguard, as well. I guess that was a true statement. He was her bodyguard, he had been looking out for her for a few years now, and he was the only one she trusted. This day had taken a turn for the worst. DAMN! It had me feeling like the universe didn't want me to come home in the first place. This had been one fucked up day.

So many thoughts were racing through my damn head. For one, where do we go from here? My Father was the backbone of the family, even though my Mom's was the glue. Imagine this scene; the two-hundred people on the outside had grown to just about double within the last two hours. If you didn't know what was going on, you would have probably thought it was an angry mob trying to get into a castle in a different day and age. Believe it or not, the people weren't doing anything crazy. Either they respected my Pops that much, or they were afraid of Mister's crew. I heard they were ruthless.

"King!" "Wassup, Mister?" "Step in the kitchen, let's talk." "Okay. Cool." As we walked into the kitchen, he started explaining to me that my Pops was killed in a prison riot by the riot squad, who were claiming that he was stabbed already when they dragged him off into the smoky clouds of tear gas which didn't sit well with Mister or me. He then explained the riot kicked off with this white supremacist group called the Aryan Nation, which was all staged to put a hit on my Pops. Rumors were that as soon as the riot cops dragged him off, they held him down while two Aryan Nation Brothers stabbed him eighteen times. My Pops was stabbed. I should've been hurting on the inside, but the truth of the matter was that I didn't feel a thing. All I could think about was killing the people who killed him because I knew he would want that.

"HEY, MISTER, I got a question for you." "Wut dat, King?" "We received the word dat my Pops was killed only about an hour ago. How are you receiving all of dis info so quickly?" It wasn't that I didn't trust Mister. I just wanted to know everything that he knew since I just found out that I was next in line to run the family criminal enterprise. So then Mister responded by saying, "We got people on the inside. I know you remember your Uncle Doc?" "Yeah, I remember him. How could I forget?"

Good Old Uncle Doc was my Pops older brother. all of the kids in the hood would call him Good Old Doc because he made it his job to make sure that all of the kids were well cared for. Then Mister went on to tell me that one of their inside guys was a CO named Charles, who was the brother of Doc's wife, Michelle. Doc paid Charles two hundred grand to leave his old job as a fireman to become a CO so that they could have an inside-outside man. The guy Charles was only one out of a few people that weren't inmates that worked for my Father, which didn't surprise me.

Mister said that Charles saw the entire riot from his tower. As soon as a full riot breaks out, the tower door automatically locks to protect the CO until the riot squad shows up. Charles also said that they shipped Doc and two other inmates close to my Father around 4am, and he didn't get to work until 10am. The phone lines didn't work until 11am, but the riot started about 10:30, assuring us that it was a setup.

As I stood there listening to Mister with tears of anger in his eyes, all I could say to him was, "Who do we kill first?" "Don't know yet, King, but as soon as we find out, they ASS IS GRASS! ***DAMN! THE KING IS DEAD*!!**"

Chapter Six

A VERBAL COMMITMENT

Kim

Gosh, one more week to graduation, then signing day is a week after that. Time is moving fast. "KIM!!!" "YES, MA'AM!" "COME ON DOWNSTAIRS AND EAT, DINNER IS READY!" "OK, I'M, COMING!"

Lord knows I love my Momma, but these last couple of weeks at the dinner table had been a nightmare due to her only thinking about herself. She's so selfish. Yesterday at dinner, all she could talk about was her new car and how her coworkers were jealous of her recent promotion and new Jeep. MAN, OH MAN, OH MAN. If she didn't stop her antics, I was going to jump out of the window. Shaking my head, I laughed out loud.

"Kim, I like the people at the University of South Carolina." Here we go again. My Mother's latest dinner tantrum was about where I should go to college and where I should play professional basketball as well. This woman was getting on my last nerve. If it wasn't for Dan, I think I would've been on the verge of losing my mind.

Dan Tolliver was the assistant principal at my high school, plus my Mom's boyfriend. Imagine all of the kids making fun of me behind my back. The only thing that probably saved me from the teasing and ridicule in my face was that I was a star athlete, and not just any star athlete, but the number 1 College recruit in the nation. I was a real one and done, which was the college terminology for a one-year college player that went straight to the pros. I would be the first woman athlete to play one year of college ball, then go straight to the WNBA. The media was calling me, "The Queen of The Hardwood", the one that would change the entire landscape of Women's Basketball and the WNBA, which will be great for the sport. Some people said that my impact would be more impactful than when LeBron James went to the NBA. I wasn't big on reading articles about myself, which I knew most people would kill for if given the opportunity.

There was this one female writer, Linda Combs, whose articles I just happen to love reading in the sports column of the Post and Courier located in Charleston, South Carolina. Linda had been writing articles about me ever since I was in middle school, but no one knew back then. I remember this article she wrote telling the world that I had arrived. It was my freshman year at North Charleston High, after the first game of the season against James Island Charter High. At the time, they were two-time back-to-back State Champs. James Island High School was good. I mean, their women's basketball program had won four State Championships out of the last six years. They were the favorite by twenty-five points, according to the Las Vegas bookmakers.

Could you blame them? Last year we were 2-12, but I wasn't on the team then, so everybody counted us out. But yes, you guessed it, we ended up winning 75-63. I scored forty-four points, pulled down fifteen rebounds, and dished out ten assists—a triple-double in my debut as a freshman. Oh, I almost forgot to mention that I had two breakaway dunks as well, and it's not every day that you see a woman basketball player dunking a basketball; thus, the legend of the Super Freshman, The Queen of The Hardwood, began. The headline read, "Kimberly Gore, The Super Freshman of North Charleston High Single-Handedly Beat Up On The Back-To-Back State Champions of James Island High." It read: *"It was a game to remember for those of us who were blessed to witness it. This six-foot,-two-inch, one- hundred-forty-pound freshman phenom dismantled the defending champions, to the likes of which I'd never seen. Kimberly put up forty-four points, fifteen rebounds, and ten assists: a triple-double for the ages. I am telling you, sports fans, Kimberly Gore is the best women's basketball player I have ever seen with my own two eyes. She's amazing! I can say this young lady is like a comet falling to earth on a crash course with the ocean. If you know third-grade science, then you already know this comet will not just make a splash, it will be a Tsunami of an impact all around the world."*

That article was the start of the good and bad things to come. Don't get me wrong, I was grateful that I'd finally found a world where my height was a bonus, but with great power comes greater responsibilities. There we go, back to the good and evil, the yin and yang. In school, I studied philosophy, so I better came to understand the nature of life by understanding that most everything in life had two parts, the yin, and the yang, a right from wrong, birth, and/or death. There's no one without the other; that's just the way life works. So, dealing with the yin part of becoming a successful ballplayer was the worst at times. You couldn't go anywhere without having to sign four of five autographs, but like I was saying, with great power comes even greater responsibility.

The next morning on the way to the bus stop, I noticed Mr. John, our bus driver, standing outside of the bus. He was about thirty minutes earlier than his usual time. My intuition told me something was different. As I approached Mr. John, he greeted me. "Good Morning, Superstar!" I greeted him back, "Good Morning Mr. John."

He nodded his head as he usually would do when we would speak to him. Mr. John then put his hand in his back pocket, pulled out The Post And Courier's copies, and smiled as he handed it to me. He said, "Would you please sign it for me saying, To John, my #1 fan."

As I unfolded the papers, I noticed a picture of me slam dunking the ball into the hoop. I looked up at Mr. John with a smile and asked him, "Is it OK for me to put my first fan?" The smile on Mr. John's face got even bigger as he said, "YES, Kimberly, that's even better."

That same morning when we arrived at school, there were at least ten news vans with cameras filming and broadcasting on the school grounds, all because of the first game of the season. As I departed the bus, all reporters and their cameramen and women started running toward the bus.

Mr. John stood up and said, "Everybody stay seated. Kimberly, you come with me!" So I did what I was told because I was starting to panic, seeing all of those people coming for me all at once. When Mr. John opened the bus door, standing in front of the door were Vice Principal Dan and five School security guards. As I exited the bus, Vice Principal Dan grabbed me by the hand and told me to run, so I did. As we ran toward the school entrance, I turned to look over my shoulder to see what was going on. I noticed that the five security guards and Mr. John were trying to hold the media back. This reminded me of the movie *Paparazzi*, so my anxiety was starting to kick in.

Once we reached the hallway, we headed straight to the guidance office, where my Mom was standing with Principal Jordan and four uniformed police officers. The scene looked like they were looking for a suspect, but they were called in by Principal Jordan, along with my Mother.

Principal Jordan expressed his concerns for my safety while I was here on school grounds due to my overnight rise to fame, plus the fifteen media vans on the campus. One of the cops started explaining that they would take care of the media by telling them that the minor, Kimberly's Mother, said she would not talk with them today.

So my Mom, being my Mom, asked the officer, "What good would that do? When we all can see that they are acting like wild animals out there!" Then the police officer responded by saying, "The Media is not allowed to talk with a minor without the parent or guardian's permission unless they want to be sued by the parents or guardian. They will not crowd her without your consent. but that doesn't mean that they won't be following you and taking pictures like the paparazzi." Then, before he and his partners turned to walk away from us, he looked at me, smiled, and then winked, and said, "Welcome to Hollywood, Superstar!" That was the beginning and the end of everyday life as I knew it, thus the yin and yang.

The first week was a struggle. I had to learn how to maneuver through my newfound success without any help. Not to mention our homecoming game was the following week, and we all expected it to be crazy due to the Administration changing the price of the admission from $5 a ticket to $25 a ticket. The game still sold out in less than five hours.

I'm not going to lie; things were moving fast and seemed to be getting out of control until Jay showed up and started informing me how to deal with the situation; I was so happy to see him. Jay started by telling me to control the media, I must invite one of them into my home for a sit-down. So we did, and who better to invite than the reporter that kicked it all off, none other than Charleston's own Linda Combs.

When Linda came to the house, she was not alone, it was six people with her, two of her colleagues from The Post and Courier, but the other three worked for ESPN News. Before the interview started, I was ready, thanks to Jay coaching me up ahead of time. Plus, Linda would be the only media member that was allowed to ask the questions, and I was ok with that.

After that interview, I was ready to take on whatever came with me loving the game of basketball. The following week, it was more of the same. The media was all over the place. It was homecoming weekend, the gym was packed inside, and outside there was a football tailgating party-like atmosphere. The game was being televised across the nation. We were playing our rivals, Burke High. They were ok, but they weren't better than us. For the last eight years, Burke High had defeated us eight years straight, but this year would be different. We defeated them with a score of 92-63. I was taken out of the game at the end of the third quarter and did not return to the game. I guess I can say I did what so many people promised, I scored thirty-seven points, pulled down thirteen rebounds, and dished out twelve assists in only three-quarters of play.

I loved playing ball just for the love of the game, but the game wasn't pure anymore. There were so many people trying to influence me on where to play my college ball. I didn't blame the people around me; it was more of the top universities and their sponsors that the Universities were in bed with. For example, the next day after the victory over Burke High, Principal Jordan called me into his office to tell me that he met with a representative for Adidas and to show me this $50,000 check that the representative gave to the school athletic program. I thought that was great until Principal Jordan told me there could be more, only if I would wear a pair of their new Adidas Viper Zooms at this upcoming game on Friday. I was totally against it due to liking how my Nikes felt.

Then Principal Jordan went on to tell me that if I wore a pair of Adidas Viper Zooms, the school would receive a 25,000 dollar donation for the athletic program every game that I wore them in. Let me remind you, this was a lot of pressure on a fifteen-year-old, but I wanted to help my school, so I agreed. Until I saw Principal Jordan show up to the fifth game of the season in a brand-new Lexus. This guy had some nerve to buy a new car before making any new improvements to the gym or any other athletic programs. The only thing that the Women's Basketball team received was a couple of uniforms with Adidas stitched on the side of them and the Adidas Viper Zooms for the entire team. The only difference was that my shoe colors were different from the rest of the team, so I would stand out.

So before game five, I decided to put back on my old uniform and my Nikes, and the other girls followed my lead. I didn't have to say anything to them; I guess they all really wanted their old personalities back. But after it was all done, we were 5-0 and getting a total overhaul for our gym, football field, cafeteria, and auditorium, plus new equipment for all of the school sports teams. That should have been done in the first place, but trust me, I was only fifteen, and I was not going to make the mistake of making any agreements with anybody in the near future without me controlling the entire situation.

That was a Moment of truth for me. I witnessed how fast money could change a person. Principal Jordan ended up taking the car back and fulfilling his obligations with the donations for the school. Only me and Principal Jordan knew about the deal he made with the Adidas's representative, and I did like Principal Jordan; he is a pretty good guy. But sometimes, even good people fall for the temptation of money, which I did understand, so I never told anyone.

That was just the beginning, even my Mother ended up getting into the act, not by choice, only by deception. When I say deception, it didn't take a lot of deceit to pull my Mother right into the water with the rest of the people that were in my life trying to persuade me to go to whatever college or corporation was footing their bills. My Mom started working for this multi-million-dollar corporation about two years ago as a technical support person at their call center. Still, she was promoted to a supervisor by the company's President and CEO, named Josh Foster. He was an Alumni of the University of South Carolina and a huge sports fan due to his big gambling habits.

Ring... Ring...

"Kimberly, get the door for me." "Who is at the door, Momma? Do you know?" "It's probably Dan! Girl, get the door." "OK."

Ring... Ring...

"HOLD ON, I'M COMING!!!" "Good evening, Kimberly." "Good evening to you, Dan." "Is your Mom in?" "Yes! She went upstairs. She will be down shortly. So Dan, what are the plans for tonight? A romantic boat ride?" Laughing, he said, "No, Kimberly, just a walk in the park." "That still sounds romantic. You guys have fun." "We will."

Dan was a real gentleman and was sweet on my Mother, as the older people used to say. When a guy liked a girl and treated her real nice, they said he was sweet on her. I don't ever recall my Mom's being so happy, and I was happy for her. Plus, did I mention that ever since Dan and my Mom's started dating, there hadn't been a single Bible study/party at our house. I was no longer confined like Cinderella on Saturday night anymore.

Ring... Ring...

I wonder who could this be at the door now? "WHO IS IT?" "It's me, Suzanne." "Oh, my bad girl. come on in." "Kimberly girl, you gotta loosen up!" "Girl, how can I? When news reporters and recruiters are watching every move that I make! Sometimes, I feel like I'm a double agent working for the United States and Russia, because I'm always looking over my shoulders." "Girl, stop being so paranoid. I be watching E! TV like all the time, and it's all a part of being a celebrity. The paparazzi be following the celebrities to different places they are trying to sneak out to. Then they jump out of the brushes and take their pictures, then sell to the highest bidder. GIRL, LET ME TAKE SOME PICS OF YOU!" "Sue, stop playing." "Girl, I'm sorry, but after three years of this stuff, I would think you were used to it by now." "I don't think I will ever get used to living like this," I said, shaking my head."

"Hey there, Mr. Tolliver!" "Hello, Suzanne! I haven't seen you at school all year, so where have you been?" "Well, I have been at home taking care of my baby and watching my lil' brother while my Mom continues to work two jobs." "I am so sorry, Suzanne, that life threw you a fastball that got in the way of you finishing your last year of high school." "It's OK, Mr. Tolliver. I did manage to go get my GED." "Well, that's great, Suzanne. Some kind of diploma is better than no diploma at all." Spoken like a real Principal, if I had to say so myself.

Being a single Mother would be something Dan Tolliver probably would never understand. My girl Sue was like a sister to me, and it did hurt my heart to find out that she was planning on dropping out of high school because her Moms couldn't afford two babysitters. Suzanne's son was almost three, and her little brother was about to turn four at the end of this month. So Sue had to miss out on her twelfth-grade year because she had to become the babysitter for both kids.

"Kimberly, Dan and I are about to leave, so don't you leave this house!" "But Momma, me and Sue had plans." "Plans to do what?" "Go to the movies." "Well, Kimberly, you and Sue will have to change y'all plans for another time." "But Mom!" "WHAT DID I SAY, KIM!" "OK, Mom" "Ann, let the girls go and hang out at the movies. You know Kimberly is heading off to college soon. It's a great idea that the girl gets a chance to hang out with each other as much as possible." "Well, Dan, if you think it would be good for them. I guess y'all girls can go. Kimberly, be home by midnight." "Thanks Momma, I will."

But I was saying thanks to Dan. Dan had always been a lifesaver. He'd been responsible for this runaway slave's freedom for the last few years. That's just a little slave humor I like to say to my friends when they start making jokes about my Momma letting me out of the house, finally.

"Girl, I see Vice Principal got your Mom's nose wide open," "Dat ain't funny, Sue." "Girl, I know! But it's true, he got her acting like a fifteen-year-old schoolgirl with her first crush on an upperclassman ." "It's called love Sue, you haven't forgotten how love goes, have you?" "NO, I haven't! Lighten up, Kim. it's me, Suzanne." "I'm sorry, Sue, I just got a lot on my mind these days, and it's been pretty hard to loosen up and have fun. Don't you know I haven't seen or heard from King in over a month?"

"No, I didn't know that girl. I'm sorry that my sorry ass baby daddy Rob set him up to get busted." "Sue, that's not it, girl. Jay told me not to mention this to anyone because it was complicated. but I'm worried about him." "Sorry, what did Jay say, Kim." "Not much, besides King's father, was killed in prison, and King is probably never coming back, and I need to just forget about him and move on with my life." "Jay said dat? Dat don't sound like the Jay I know!" "I know, right, and that's the main reason that I'm so worried about King because my intuition is telling me that something just ain't right. he's not answering my calls or returning my voicemails."

"So, did you ask Jay where he was at?" "Yes, Jay said he was back in Alabama." "So, what are you planning on doing to see if he's ok?." "I will come up with something because I truly believe there is more to Jay telling me to forget about him. Sue girl, I don't understand why Jay wouldn't want to talk to me about his cousin when he knows that King and I are close. Girl, I gotta find him." "Kim, I would suggest you hire a private investigator, but you haven't signed any of the contracts yet."

"I know, right! But I got a plan, and speaking of a contract, when are you planning on finishing those online agent certification classes?" "Girl, I got time. You still have one year of college ball to play before you turn pro." "OK, Sue, I want you to have this job of being my agent, so I won't leave you behind or end up having to take care of your grown butt. Plus, signing day is a few days away, and you know the world will be waiting and anticipating my decision of which college I am going to be attending."

Signing Day

"Hello everyone, this is John Rocker from ESPN News, broadcasting live here at North Charleston High School located in Charleston, South Carolina. Awaiting and anticipating "THE QUEEN OF THE HARDWOOD" Kimberly Gore's decision on which of these three-top division 1A powerhouse colleges will win the half a billion-dollar lottery, due to the television revenue and new endorsement deals they'll receive, just because Kimberly Gore is attending their University. Let me add that Kimberly Gore did give Duke University a verbal commitment. Still, there are two others which are The University of Notre Dame and the University of Connecticut. This is a very exciting time for all three of these universities, and I would like to say I wish them all the best in this Mega Sweepstakes."

This had been a long three-year process. The media had been all over the gym throughout the entire day, so the time had come for me to let the world know where I would be attending my one-year of college.

"Hello! My name is Kimberly Gore, and first of all, I would like to thank everyone for coming out today. After my decision, I know you all will have many questions about the college I chose. I will take a few questions, and that will be it! OK, everyone, I will be attending, *PAUSE!* ALABAMA STATE UNIVERSITY!"

After I made my decisions, the crowd was stunned. It was so quiet that you could hear a pin drop on the floor. But the quietness only lasted for about five seconds. After that, it became a frenzy of media members screaming and raising their hands for the few questions that I had promised.

"KIMBERLY!!! KIMBERLY!!! KIMBERLY!!!"

"You there, with the white blouse, go ahead with your question!" "Thanks, Kimberly. This is

Michelle Evans with The Undefeated News & Sports; I have a two-part question. This decision caught everyone off-guard. So when did you make this decision, and who else, if anyone, knew besides you?"

"Well Michelle, to answer your first question, I made this decision two weeks ago, and for question two, only two other people that knew, and those people were Coach Keisha Johnson of the ASU Hornets Women's Basketball Program, and my best friend and soon-to-be Agent, Suzanne Richardson."

"Next question, the guy in the tan blazer!" "Hello, Kimberly, and thanks for the opportunity. I am Timothy Taylor, and I am here on behalf of ESPN 2 Radio. It is true that no one saw this coming for miles, but out of all of the division A1 colleges in the country with bigger platforms, why did you choose Alabama State University?"

"Good question Timothy, but to answer that question and do not quote me on this, but we all know that I don't have to have a huge platform to get you guys' and ladies' attention. That was done my freshman year of high school here at North Charleston. So I'm saying that just to say, all I have to do is to continue working hard on my game and keep putting up triple-doubles, and everything else will fall in place. Now, to answer the question at hand, the reason I decided to go to Alabama State University because it's an HBCU, or Historically Black College and University, which fits me well because I'm African American. By attending ASU, I will be able to use my platform to help better black communities, and that is where my heart is." "Next and final question!"

"KIMBERLY!!!!" "OVER HERE!!!" "OVER HERE!!!" "KIMBERLY!!!" "KIMBERLY!!!" "KIMBERLY!!!!"

"The guy in the corner, in the very back, with the red shirt on." "Hi, Ms. Kimberly, I am

Mark Madison, here with the North Carolina News, Weather, and Sports. My question is that I would like to know, along with all of the good people in Durham, North Carolina, what happen to your commitment to Duke University?!" "Mark, it was a verbal commitment! Thank you all for coming out."

Chapter Seven

VENGEFUL THOUGHTS

BEEP…BEEP…..BEEP….

"Damn, it's morning already." As I rolled over to shut off the alarm clock, I was kind of surprised at how well I slept last night compared to the night before. The day before, all I did was toss and turn all night. I could not get the images or sounds from out of my head of those domestic pigs crunching on bones and human flesh. This was the second body within two weeks that I had to watch vanish from the face of the earth. The first was one of the two correctional officers that dragged my Pops off and held him down while a couple inmates stabbed him to death.

The first hit was led by the Queen of this family, my Mother. I had no idea what was going on. *THE NIGHT BEFORE,* all I was told was that a tailor would be here at 10am the next morning to tailor me a suit because there was a funeral we had to attend at around 1pm. So that day, me, my Moms, and Mister stepped into this new model black Cadillac Escalade which were accompanied by three other black-on-black CTS-V Cadillacs, which are luxury and speed all in one. As we arrived at the chapel connected to the funeral home, I noticed very few cars in the parking lot. As the gate started to open up at the back of the funeral home, I started thinking that this must be a private funeral.

As we pulled up to the door and everyone started to exit the truck, standing on each side of the double doors, were these two guys dressed in all black. But another guy was standing there as well. He stood about five-feet-nine-inches, average size, and weight, around 165 pounds. He was standing in front of them wearing a white jumpsuit. As we approached him, he greeted us with a head nod. As he turned to walk inside, we followed closely behind him. I had never been in the back of a funeral home, where they prepare the bodies for a funeral, and man, I tell you, it was some creepy shit. Seeing five dead people lying lifeless on tables. After we walked through the dead bodies and started to turn the corner, there was this white guy in a blue and black uniform lying on the floor with his feet and hands heavily wrapped with duct tape. By looking at him, he had taken a vicious beating to his face and head, but he was still breathing.

I guess it was a funeral of sort, this guy by the name of Mike's funeral. Mike was one of the two correctional officers that were involved in killing my Pops. So what my Mom's had planned for him, I was on board with one hundred percent of the way. As I looked him in his face, I noticed a single teardrop from his eye. I then went into a flashback of this gangster rapper named Scarface; his video started playing in the back of my mind for a split second, "I have never seen a man cry 'til I seen a man die."

No one said a word. My Mom's gave the order, and the two guys dressed in all black picked him up off the floor and shoved him into the cremation machine. He was cremated alive, which had to be a horrible death.

After the body was turned into ashes, the guy in the white jumpsuit emptied the cremation machine with Mike's ashes, loaded them in a five-gallon bucket, and took them outside to this Spanish guy, who was out back planting a new flower bed. So, Mike would be used as pottery soil by the looks of things and reincarnated as a yellow daisy.

The second hit was my call on this inmate from Greenville, Alabama, named Joseph Jenkins. He also played a role in my Pops' murder. He was one of the stabbers. Joseph was serving time on two life sentences for a double vehicle homicide while driving under the influence of alcohol. But at the time, Joseph had only served five years, a quarter of the time on one of the two life sentences, and was not really eligible for parole until he served at least seven to eight years. I'm sure he would have been denied parole due to him not doing enough time on his sentences, along with the protest from the families, which could have gone for twenty, thirty, forty, or even fifty years. Who's to say?

So, I did the work of what most inmates would look at as a blessing from God. I made one phone call to a friend that worked on the parole board. Just like that, a week later, he was granted parole, and the prison gates parted for him as the Red Sea parted for Jesus. I don't think this fool had any idea that the day he was being released from prison would be his last day living. The parole board arranged for him to be released at 6:30am Monday morning and have a car pick him up at 6:45am to take him to the bus stop. From there, he would be heading to Greenville, Alabama. He never made it to Greenville. He was kidnapped by The Body Snatchers, these three crazy-ass brothers from the bayou of New Orleans. These brothers were semi-race car drivers but very dangerous and carried a reputation for making people disappear in the bayou swamps.

The Body Snatchers met me, Mister, and two other crew members at this cabin, where they were told to deliver the package. The place was located ten plus miles off the main road. This cabin was heavily surrounded by trees. It was owned by my family and run by Mister's uncle, Lonnie, who raised and sold domestic and wild pigs to other pig farmers.

This was my first-time meeting Lonnie, but he assured me that he would make this inmate Joseph pay for what he did to my Pops. Plus, make him disappear for good, where he would never be found. I then assured him that it would be a bonus in it for him if he could make him disappear right in front of my eyes. It wasn't that I didn't trust Lonnie. I was fairly new to this mafia lifestyle, so I needed to soak up as much game as possible, and I was willing to pay extra for the lessons. Understand I was the Boss, but there were still rules to the game, and that was the game should be sold, not told. The Body Snatchers arrived with

Joseph, who was hog-tied and wrapped in plastic from his feet to his neck. As Mister and Lonnie picked Joseph up out of the back seat of this Silver 1984 Chevrolet Monte Carlo SS, identical to the car that Mister owned, but just a different color, I walked over to the car to meet the brothers from the bayou. There were only two of the three. We shook hands, then we talked for about ten minutes. Just long enough to know and recognize one another, so whenever we met again, we wouldn't be total strangers. I told Rick to pay them so that they could be on their way back to New Orleans.

After seeing The Body Snatchers off, I turned my focus back to this guy Joseph. I watched Lonnie and Mister drag him off through the fields where the pig pens were located. When we reached the pens, the smell was pretty bad, something I wasn't used to smelling. Once again, I was focused, waiting on Lonnie to show me how he was planning on making this coward Joseph disappear from the face of the earth without a trace. Lonnie took out this Rambo-looking knife, leaned over to Joseph, and started making some minor cuts on both of Joseph's legs. Once the blood began to run down Joseph's knees, Mister and Lonnie picked him up in the air, then threw him into the pen.

As soon as the first pig started chewing on one of his bloody legs, the other pigs turned around and started swarming him like a beehive. It was like something straight out of a horror flick. It took less than two hours, and when the pigs were through feasting, there were no signs of this guy Joseph. This was gruesome and amazing at the same time. Plus, after seeing that, I was going on a no pig diet for as long as I lived.

I had only been head of the family for a month. This Mob life had really changed what I thought my life would end up being something that most people would never know and can only live through books, documentaries, and movies. Not me, and the strange part about all of this was that I think I was starting to enjoy the rush of this superspeedway lifestyle. It's just something about the feeling of living above the law that made me want to live this way for as long as I was on God's green earth and be willing to take whatever consequences of this lifestyle as a Mob Boss.

Being a Mob Boss meant I must watch and pay one hundred percent attention to every detail of whatever was happening in front of me and more so behind me. Because there were people in my organization, and people on the outside looking in, who were trying to take me out so that they could take over the many companies that my family built from the ground up, illegally and by any means necessary. As I speak, my family was at war with a couple of families from the bottom half of Alabama. Those families were the Knight Family and the Collins Family. Both families were conspiring together so that they could take over the empire my father built, from farming to real estate, which included buying and developing commercial properties, along with dozens of other lucrative businesses.

I was told there were rules to war when my family donned me the new Boss of all Bosses. But I didn't think the Collins family ever got the memo. Rule number one, which is the most important rule when it came down to war, was no killing of any women or children in the time of war. I didn't think any of the rules applied to the Collins family. They were descendants of the Ku Klux Klan, or the KKK, a racist white supremacist group of individuals who didn't want to accept that the South lost the American Civil War and still thought they were superior to every other race on this planet.

These muthafuckas, just the other day, killed Stan's sixteen-year-old son right in front of his high school by crushing his Ford Focus into a tree using a damn dump truck that had a Confederate license plate. That was only one of the many tragedies my family had to face in the last couple of weeks, so I had to give the order that all kids connected to this family needed to start homeschooling immediately. After the death of Stan Jr., we could not afford to lose any more kids. They were the future of this family, and I would not sit around and wait on the Collins family to pick them off one by one. That wasn't going to happen on my watch as Boss of this family.

The Collins owned fifty percent of the farming industry in Alabama and came to my Pops a few years back trying to buy him out of his thirty-five percent. Still, he turned down their offer because he knew the value of growing and producing your own food by farming. My Pops always believed in growing fruit, vegetables, and farm animals the all-natural way. Plus, it's a lot of money in farming. My family had grossed a little over two million dollars annually for the last five years. The Collins wanted our land, and it seemed like they would go to any extent to obtain it, but we were not selling. These were some evil Muthafuckas. They kidnapped one of our best farmers, chopped off his right hand with an electric saw, and then told him to tell me that there wouldn't be any farmers alive to farm our lands if we didn't sell. I never took threats lightly, and I wasn't about to start now. I had the money and all of the resources I needed to keep my people safe until I could develop a plan to end this war.

I was told that my family had been competing with the Collins family before I was born, but never to the point where they were willing to go to war over something that was rightfully ours. My Mom's told me that she had a feeling one of the only two bad decisions that my Pops made would come back to kill him one day. The first one was when he was a teenager. He was shot multiple times, but he ended up pulling through that. My Mom's said that my Pops made a huge mistake by not killing his cousin; Money Hungry Robert is what people called him. Robert Knight should've been killed for stealing tens of thousands of dollars from the family, along with making some shady back deals with the Collins without my Pops' permission. Instead of killing Robert, he took his title of the Underboss. He banished him, his family, and whoever wanted to follow him to Greenville, Alabama. He was not allowed to visit any of the city above Montgomery. Yes, I would have to agree with my Mom's due to my Pops still giving Robert his permission to do business in the lower parts of Alabama. Plus, supplying him with the resources at a seventy-thirty split, which was plenty enough for Money Hungry Robert to start building his swampland paradise. I think my Pops underestimated Robert by having him work the swampy parts of Alabama, knowing that this guy was a real snake. I wished my Pops would have killed him. He would still be alive today.

    I couldn't sit around thinking about the what ifs while these two motherfucking families were trying to muscle their way in on my family's legacy. I guess it was time to meet up with Cousin Robert so that we could put an end to all of this bloodshed, once and for all. So I called Robert that night to let him know that we were still family, and there was no reason we couldn't work something out. At first, Robert responded by saying that my father owed him a decade of back pay from the seventy-thirty, which should have been fifty-fifty, plus the amount of money he would have made if he was still the Underboss and not banished. I truly thought that was ridiculous and a slap in the face, but to show good faith, I agreed to half of his demands, which rounded off to nine million, give or take a dollar. I also had to give him back his title of Underboss and lift all bands or restrictions from his family. Robert also asked for a fifty-fifty split on this new forty-million-dollar land development deal my Pops signed a month before his death, which was all willed to me. So I agreed to his terms, as long as he agreed that he would stop working with the Collins and move forward with the healing process of our families.

My Mom's was pissed. She was so pissed that as soon as I told her about the arrangement I made with Cousin Robert, she immediately said she thought I was following in my father's footsteps. Then she went on to say she would pray that the outcome would be different this time around and that she was going on a vacation to Bora-Bora, French Polynesia, for six weeks. She added that she'd pray I was still alive when she got back. I then told her that I would be awaiting her arrival back in the states and not to worry about me, just enjoy the vacation, I would be fine.

Chapter Eight

A REAL FAMILY REUNION

Six weeks had passed since I made the transfer of fifteen million into Robert Knight's bank account while agreeing to make him a full-time partner in this one project of land and development. The development consisted of sixty new homes, surrounded by three ponds and a full-length shopping center, which would soon be occupied by the likes of a Super Walmart, movie theater, Dave and Buster's, two gas stations, and six different high-end restaurants. This was what you call building from the ground up, literally.

RING...RING...

"HELLO!" "King, are you up out of bed yet?" "Yeah, Mister, I'm up early every morning. You should know by now that I don't sleep well, and I'm up two or three days at a time every week." "OK, cool, I gotta remember that, but I've sent Maine and eight of my best Souljas to pick your Moms up from the airport and bring her straight to the land development construction site. Queen should arrive within the next two King." "OK, Mister, let me jump in the shower, and we'll be there within the next hour. Is everything still on schedule to happen as planned?" "Yep, everything is still a go, BOSS!" "Man, what I told you about calling me boss? We brothers, you can still call me King." "I know, just fucking with you this morning." "Very funny, dude."

This was a big deal for my family and me. Developing a whole community with all of the luxuries within walking distance was always a dream of my Pops'. He wasn't able to see it all the way through due to his death, but I think he would be proud of the steps I was taking by following in his footsteps. My Mom's didn't like the fact that I split this deal with my father's killer just to stop the war between the two families, but like Jay-Z said on his 4:44 album, *"Nobody wins when the family feuds,"* which I truly believed. Therefore, I felt it was for the greater good. Both families would survive with the least casualties as possible. I guess this meeting with the heads of the two families was somewhat of a family reunion. My intuition told me that by reuniting with the Knights, the Collins would no longer pursue this war, knowing that they didn't have enough resources or manpower. Rule number one in the art of war is what Tupac used to love to say, "don't go to war until you get your money right."

So the Knights turning their backs on the Collins left the Collins with no other choice but to withdraw from the war. This war had taught me that money and power were the only things that mattered to the people on top, and they would do anything to stay on top. Even if they had to kill their blood. I knew that Robert would stab me in the back the first chance he got so that he could become the Big Boss of the family. I refused to let that happen; therefore, I must continue to stay ten steps ahead of him in this chess match.

"Maine, how much time do we have before we reach the construction site?" "About fifty-five minutes or so, Mrs. Wright." "OK, Maine, tell the driver to step on it, so we can cut the time in half. My son said that he got me an early Birthday present." "Yes, ma'am! Mark, HIT IT! I need you to cut the time in half."

As Mister and I pulled up to the center of the neighborhood, part of the development site, I noticed that the project manager did as he was told. He'd broken ground on the eight acres of land that I was building my Mom's house on, but we weren't going to pour the foundation until today.

Shortly after we arrived, the Mayor pulled up in a gray stretch Lincoln Continental Town Car, accompanied by two motorcycle sheriff's deputies. I invited the Mayor to this meeting to let him know that my family would still support him in next year's election, the same as my Pops would have done.

"I am sorry for your loss, son. How are you holding up?" "I'm holding fine, Mr. Mayor." "That is great to hear. Your father was a good man, King, and I truly regret he is not here to see you continue to put his dream in motion. He would be proud of you." "Thanks, Mayor, I truly believe that, but we can get back to the sentimental part of our new relationship later." "I agree Son, yes, you are your father's son. You don't deal with emotions when doing business, and that's what I liked about your father. I think we are going to be the best of friends." "Only time will tell, Mayor!" "Call me Johnny, son" "Ok Johnny, but do me the same favor and stop calling me son. I don't need another father!" "Understood, King" "Thanks again, Johnny, for coming out to support my Pops dreams along with seeing my vision."

"King, if it weren't for your father, I would probably be in jail or dead, it's only fair to come out and support his son the same way he supported me all these years. Plus, a one-million-dollar check will cancel a lot of plans on anyone's busy schedule, you know what I mean." "Yes I do. Mister, pay the man." Mister walked to the trunk of his car and pulled out a duffel bag containing one million dollars in cold hard cash, all hundred-dollar bills. Mister handed the bag to the Mayor, then the Mayor handed it off to one of the deputies, who then placed the bag in the Lincoln Continental trunk. "So, King!" "Yes, Johnny." "Is this plan of yours fool-proof?" "Trust me, Johnny, do your part, and we will take care of the rest. Here comes the guest of honor, as we speak."

My cousin Robert Knight pulled up in three black Chevy Suburban's with his normal crew of eight bodyguards. They always accompanied him on all of his outdoor activities, from going to the parks to coming to meetings, which would start as soon as my Mom's arrived. Robert was also accompanied by his wife, Melissa Knight, and their two sons, Leon and George. Leon was the oldest of the Knight boys and the true heir to the Knight empire, but he has been outcast by his parents due to his sexual preference. Leon was bisexual, and that didn't sit well with his Mother Melissa, who decided to take him out of their will and make George the heir to the throne. Melissa Knight was a real control freak and a dominatrix. Now, look at the kettle calling the pot black.

Rumors said that Melissa was into all types of kinky sex acts. I'm talking about having two or three people tied or chained up in the estate's basement, men and women, all having one big orgy. This damn family was all fucked up. There had also been rumors that Melissa's two boys were the product of her sex cult and that Robert Knight was not the boys' biological father. He couldn't have any kids, according to his first wife and the doctor's report she had on him when they were trying to have a kid. George was Robert's favorite out of the two boys. George was Robert's second in command, while Leon had to work two part-time jobs and pay most of his college tuition.

"COUSIN KING!!! Good to see you. Where is your beautiful Mother? Ain't she a part of this meeting?" "Yes, she is a part of this meeting; she should be arriving soon." "Ok, cousin, but you know time is money, and you know I love me some money ." "Cousin Robert, have you met Mayor Johnny White?" "Mayor White? He looks black to me! Just kidding, Mayor, nice to finally meet you. I be hearing a lot of good things about you!" "Oooh really, like what?" "Just the normal things, like you, are a great guy, but you will need twice as many campaign donations to win this upcoming election.

I also heard that you are old news and that this graduate student from Auburn University will soon become the new face of this growing city, making me think that I need to align my family with him over you." "HEY, ROBERT! Don't you think you are being too harsh on the Mayor?" "Hold on, King, I can fight my own battles! Look here, you *ASSHOLE*. *Don't* let this thousand-dollar suit and these glasses fool your ass. Nigga, I'm from the west side of town, and I don't play that disrespectful shit, you fake ass wanna be John Gotti looking muthafucka!!!"

"Mayor, why the bad language?" "See it's times like this that I thank God for my past lifestyle, which I don't regret. Because who knew in my line of work I would have to deal with snake muthafuckas like you! But I want you to know that I have seen dozens of people like you come and go. Some are serving life sentences in the federal penitentiary, and others in an early grave. So you be careful with the way you talk to people because you probably gonna need all of the friends you can get!" "Well Mister Mayor, I plan on being around for a long time, so get used to it. Let me introduce you to my family. This here is my never seems to age, beautiful wife, Melissa Knight, and our two sons, Leon and George Knight." "Nice to meet you all."

After that awkward ass greeting between Mayor White and my asshole of a Cousin Robert Knight, my Mom's convoy finally arrived. I knew this meeting would get a lot worse before it could go in the direction that I was planning on taking it.

Robert was on the list of the most hated people in the world in my Moms' eyes. She wanted him dead, and she wasn't the only one that felt that way. I wasn't sure how this meeting would end. As my Mom's exited the vehicle, I walked over to greet her. "Hello Mother, how was the trip back?" "It was ok, I guess. So let's go and take care of this meeting so I can get home." "Yes ma'am, this won't take long."

"Hell, Amber! Girl, you don't look a day out of high school." "It's Mrs. Wright to you, Robert!" "Don't be like that Amber, we're family, and this here is a family reunion. We haven't seen one another in years." "Hi Amber, I'm sorry about the loss of your husband." "Bitch, bye! Don't act like you don't know! Don't you dare bring him up, neither one of you! See King, I told you not to make this deal with these tyrants, Standing here on your fathers' dream, making a mockery of his death, which they played a part in." "Come on, Amber. we had nothing to do with it, but I heard that the

Collins family was responsible for Marcus's demise." "Well, Robert, you know what they say, a lie can travel halfway around the world while the truth is still getting its pants on, but we're not here to go back and forth about the past. I'm more focused on the future.

Today, I bring these two families together to celebrate my Pops' dream. So the arguments will stop here and now!" "I see the son is a lot smarter than his father was." This muthafucka Robert didn't have an off button, but this day was to celebrate my Pops' achievements, and I wasn't going to let this asshole steal me or my Moms' joy. "Oh, Momma, I forgot to tell you that this entire lot that we're standing on is where we will be building your new house." "King, didn't I tell you I was fine where I was, that I wasn't moving, and there's nothing you can do to change my mind!" "Come on, King, I know you didn't bring my family and me out here so you could try to convince your Mother to move?" "No, I didn't bring you and your family out here to help me convince my Momma to move out of the projects. This is a real family reunion. It's a celebration. I also have your early birthday present, Momma, which I know will change your mind." "Ok, son, so where is it?" "Mister, give it to her!"

Mister pulled out his gun and hit the first bodyguard with three shots, one shot to the face and the other two shots, two to the chest. At the same time, two more bodyguards fell to the ground, both hit with long-distance headshots, courtesy of my guardian angel Todd Smith.

Robert turned to his other five bodyguards and yelled out, "KILL THEM!!! KILL THEM ALL!!!" His bodyguards didn't follow his command, and that's when he fell to his knees and started to beg for his life. George tried to run but was soon tackled by two of the bodyguards, brought back, and placed on his knees next to Robert and Melissa. "COME ON KING, DON'T DO DIS. WE FAMILY!!!" "We're not family, family don't cross family and trust me you crossed the wrong one!! Now Mister, duct tape their hands behind their backs." "PLEASE….. COUSIN, I WILL GO BACK TO GREENVILLE AND NEVER COME BACK!!!" "One of those statements is true. You won't be coming back ever in life. NOW MISTER, TAPE THIS LOUDMOUTH MUTHAFUCKA'S MOUTH SHUT!"

"PLEASE!……."

I pulled out my Glock 40, pointed it at George's head, and pulled the trigger. His body dropped like a sack of potatoes. I called my Mom's over to execute Robert's wife Melissa the same way they did my Pops. My Momma fired off two quick headshots, then turned the gun on Robert, but I stopped her, gave her a kiss on the cheek, and said, "Happy early birthday, Moms. I'm going to bury him alive." She smiled and started to walk towards Mayor White to greet him.

"So Leon, once Robert is gone, all of his belongings will belong to you." "All I want is his brand-new BMW M8. I need an upgrade on my vehicle and the job that you promised me when all of this was over. I want to make my own money. You can do whatever you feel is best with theirs." "Ok Leon, I understand why you feel this way, but there are a few things I must do for you." "What's that, King?" "Let me buy you another BMW M8 for your male friend so that you two can have matching rides and also pay for your child a full ride to whatever college his or her heart desires." "Ok King, I would like that. you got a deal."

"OK, MAINE! Let's bury this piece of shit of a family before the contractor arrives to pour the foundation to the house." "WILL DO, BOSS!"

I gave Mister the order to throw Robert into the hole alive first, while Maine took the bulldozer and scooped up the other five dead bodies, along with a bunch of dirt, and started filling the hole until all of the bodies were completely buried. All I could do was stand there watching as I imagined Robert taking his last breath, which I knew was a cruel death but fitting for all of the hurt this damn guy brought into so many lives, especially Leon's. No kid should have to go through what he had to with his parents. So, if not for Leon's help, none of this would have been so simple.

One of the young guys working for Maine was dating Leon's soon-to-be baby momma's sister. She was running off at the mouth about this guy from Greenville, Alabama, sneaking up here to see her sister in her dorm room at Alabama State University. So I had the youngin' bring his girlfriend to me and gave her five thousand to pick the person's picture out that she said was named Leon from Greenville, and she did just that. It was like hitting five out of six numbers of the mega millions jackpot. You might not win the whole thirty-two million, but you'll get a portion of it. So I had Maine and a few of his guys go on-campus and wait on him to come to see his soon-to-be baby mamma, then bring him to me unharmed. Which they did.

Leon was not a violent person, as far as I knew, due to the information I had received within my reports of him. Therefore, I had no reason to force him into the trunk of a car. Maine did as he was told, and that was to approach Leon to tell him that I requested his presence. I knew Leon felt like he had no choice in the matter, which was true, but he was a smart guy and agreed to meet with me without causing a scene, which probably would have gotten him killed.

When he arrived, we sat down and talked for hours. He told me how he was going to Community College in Greenville. He wanted to become an interior designer and decorator. He had been working two part-time jobs for the last three years to pay his college tuition. He hated his parents for turning their backs on him when he was only twelve years old because they found out that he was bi and in love with one of his high school classmates. They were still in a committed relationship.

I felt bad for Leon, but I felt worse for the families that had lost loved ones because of this war that his dad helped start. I knew I had to come up with a plan to end this war and fast. That's when I decided to make Leon an offer. I told him I needed him to bug Robert's office and his car, and in return, I would pay off all of his student loans, plus pay his last year of college. And, as soon as he completes his degree, I would give him a seven-figure contract to do all of the interior designing and decorating in all sixty houses on this new land and development project, which he gladly agreed to, under one other condition, that was to let him out of the family business completely. He said he didn't want any part of the Mafia lifestyle. I knew where Leon's mindset was at the time. If a person had two choices, to work for a boss or become the boss of their world, most people would choose door

#2. I agreed to Leon's terms, and that was the start of the fall of the Knight family.

Chapter Nine

THIS MUST END NOW

RING... RING... RING...

I wonder who this is ringing my damn doorbell like they have lost their fuckin mind. "Who is it?" "IT'S ME, MISTER. OPEN UP THE DOOR, KING!!!" "What's the deal, Mister. What's wrong?" "TURN ON THE NEWS, CHANNEL 8, WAKA!

So I did just as Mister suggested that I do with such urgency to see that it was a live shooter on the ASU campus. Mister explained that Leon called and told him that he got an anonymous phone call around ten this morning, stating that they knew he played a part in his family's disappearance and that they were not coming after him, but his family instead. After Mister asked him what family they could be talking about, Leon told him his boyfriend and his soon-to-be baby's mother were all the family he had. His boyfriend was with him now, but his baby's mother was in class at ASU. Before Mister and his crew could get on campus, MPD had already blocked off the entire campus. The shooter had already done his damage!

BREAKING NEWS LIVE: "I am Jack Rivers with WAKA News, coming to you live on the campus of Alabama State University, here in Montgomery, Alabama! There has been a shooting in the Science Building right behind me, and my sources are telling me that this shooter is still in the classroom and has three hostages as well!

Hold on, folks!!! My sources just told me that there were eight people shot, two dead, and the other six rushed to the hospital with severe injuries from gunshot wounds. My sources tell me that one of the three hostages is none other than the All-American, All-World Standout Freshman Women's Basketball Star, Kimberly Gore, and Professor Albert Gray, and another student Christina Thomas. My sources tell me that Kimberly Gore has been shot once in the shoulder. She stopped the shooter from shooting a classmate by the name of Lisa Noles. Lisa Noles happens to be six months pregnant. Kimberly Gore can add Hero to her resume, as well. This is truly one special young lady, and all of our prayers go out to her, Professor Gray, and Christina Thomas."

I couldn't believe what I was watching on the news. Kimberly was here in town, attending Alabama State University. Now, she was a hostage of the Collins. Thank the Great Creator that the Collins had no idea that I knew Kimberly. If they did, she would-be dead-on sight. I had to act fast to save her and the others.

"MISTER!!!" "YES, BOSS!" "Call Pig in Greenville and tell him to go and snatch up the Collins' kid and bring him to me! He's at baseball practices. Pig knows where it is, and Mister, don't forget to tell Pig that the kid might have more than two bodyguards with him. Take at least eight to ten guys with him and kill any and everybody trying to stand in the way. Plus, tell them I need him alive, and I NEED THIS DONE LIKE

YESTERDAY! THIS MUST END NOW!!!" "I'm on it, ASAP!"

In the midst of all of this madness, I've had to live through for the last five months or so. I thought about Kimberly a lot. But my heart wouldn't allow me to bring our two lives together. I hadn't been watching any news or sports programs lately to find out where she intended to play college ball. The universe had a strange way of bringing people back together. Like people say, if it's meant to be, it would be. Here we go again. Please let it be some good news this time.

LIVE BREAKING NEWS: Once again, I am Jack Rivers with WAKA Channel 8 Local News, here live at Alabama State University, where there has been a campus shooting. The death total is now four, and the other four are fighting for their lives. Again, we here at WAKA send our prayers out to all the students and their families on this tragic day that will not be forgotten. This is a sad, sad day for the Hornet Nation. Standing here with me now is Lisa Noles, one of the students that happened to get away from the shooter with the help of her classmate Kimberly Gore.

"Hello, Lisa! I am Jack Rivers here with WAKA news. Can you tell our viewers what happened up there in the classroom, and how did Kimberly Gore help you escape?" "Yes, Kimberly did put her life on the line for me! SHE'S A HERO! She saved my unborn child and me. The shooting happened so fast, I happened to be sitting in the fourth row when this bald-headed white guy wearing a long brown trench coat stepped in the classroom doorway and pulled out from underneath his coat an assault rifle, aimed it in my direction, and started shooting. I was in shock and couldn't move until I heard a voice saying out loud, "run, Lisa, run…". I looked up, and I saw some of my classmates lying on the floor bleeding. Kimberly was wrestling with this guy, trying to take the rifle away from him, while looking in my direction, telling me to run. so I did just that."

"Thank you, Lisa, for sharing your story with the world and giving the viewers and us a real-time vision of today's tragic event. Remember world, you heard it here first, and I am Jack Rivers with WAKA News signing off!"

Once I got my hands on the Collins' boy, I knew for a fact that Bob Collins would do just about anything to get him back unharmed. I wasn't a monster like his ass, but this needed to be done to stop this guy from hurting anybody else. Truly I wasn't a monster, but if that fucking shooter hurt Kimberly, I would erase the entire bloodline, dating back to the 1800s, including first and second cousins.

Ring…

"Hello!" "They got him, BOSS!" "Ok, Mister, great news! Give me the quick run down." "Ok, Pig said it was only two guards, so they didn't have to fire off a single round. Our guess is that the bodyguards decided since they were outnumbered ten to two, there was no reason to play the hero." "Tell Pig great job, and he and his crew will be rewarded later. It's time to end this shit now! Let me call this Muthafucka Bob!"

RING... RING...

"YOU SON OF A BITCH, WHERE'S MY BOY! IF YOU LAY YOUR FILTHY HANDS ON HIM, I WILL FIND YOU AND CUT YOU A MILLION TIMES WITH A RAZOR BLADE AND STAND THERE AND WATCH YOU BLEED OUT LIKE A PIG."

"Hold on, Bob, is that any way to talk to the guy that holds your future in his hand?" "NO! I'm sorry, what do you want me to do?" "Ok, that's more like it. First, I need you to call off that shooter on the campus of ASU. Tell him to turn himself in now, without hurting another soul. If not, I will feed your son to the gators in the Louisiana swamp. You got five minutes!" It only took three minutes. I noticed another Breaking News flash.

LIVE BREAKING NEWS: "Hi, I am Jack Rivers coming to you live once again, and I am with WAKA Channel 8 News here in Montgomery, Alabama! It looks like the MPD SWAT team is about to move in on the shooter, as we all witnessed someone up on the second floor, where the hostages are being held, started waving a white shirt out of the window. Then, just seconds later, the assault rifle came out the same window. I do not know, but normally in the movies, when someone waves a white towel or shirt, it means that person is offering a sign of surrender or defeat. We can all see that the cops are not taking any chances. They are in their full SWAT gear moving in as I speak. We will stay here live to bring you real-time updates of this story as we wait patiently on the SWAT team.

My sources have confirmed that the assault rifle tossed from the second floor and a handgun are the weapons used in today's shooting. HOLD ON! That looks like the SWAT team coming out of the building with the suspect with his hands behind his back. Now, one of the SWAT members are waving at the paramedics along with the first responders' Fire Department. I think it's safe to say that the guy in the back of the SWAT car is the shooter, and everyone is relieved that he's been apprehended. We are still holding our breaths, hoping that all three of the hostages are alive and well.

"Coming in now from my sources, they're telling me that Kimberly Gore, the All-World Women's Basketball Star, has been shot in her left shoulder, which is her shooting arm, and has been placed on a stretcher. She is in the emergency vehicle headed to the hospital. I was told that Professor Albert Gray and student Christine Thomas are safe without any bodily harm. Our prayers go out to her and the rest of the families of ASU. Here come the paramedics, with Kimberly strapped down on the stretcher, rushing to the emergency vehicle as fast as they can. They are now off to the hospital with several cop cars and news vans trailing close behind them. Once again, I am Jack Rivers with WAKA Channel 8 Local News signing off!"

RING…

"HELLO!!! I did what you asked of me. The shooter did what you wanted, so where is my son?" He is with a trusted associate of mine." "AN ASSOCIATE? WHAT THE HELL, MAN!!! KING, AN ASSOCIATE? COME ON, MAN, HE'S ONLY TWELVE." "Calm down my friend" "I'm not your fuckin friend, you nigga. You have my fuckin child with a fuckin' associate who is probably sodomizing my boy as we speak!"

"You listen to me, you colonizing, backstabbing, lying, manipulating, wet dog smelling muthafucka! Your son is in good hands! trust me. He's safer than you are right now, with that purple ass Liberace flannel shirt on." "So you are spying on me?" "No Bob, I wouldn't call it spying. Generals call it the art of war. Knowing where your enemies are and what they are doing at all times is only a small part of it." "So, you think you are smarter than all of the bosses. You barely have hair around your balls, kid!"

"That might be true on both ends. I'm smarter, plus having hair around your balls doesn't make you a man; having big balls do! Bob, this must end now! Meet me at the same location that you used to meet up with Robert Knight, and you can bring me a gift for a truce between our families. The ball is in your court. Plus, it's common courtesy to bring someone a gift that is bringing you one. See you in an hour!"

Before getting on I-65 south heading towards Greenville, Mister and I met up with four of my newly recruited guys at this safe house. It was located on the outskirts of the city, in a small town called Hope Hull. We had to pick up the Collins kid and put him in the car with us. Going into this meeting, there was only one plan, and that was to come out alive. Mister and I loaded up the Collins kid in the back seat of Mister's 1984 Chevrolet Monte Carlo SS. This car was crazy fast, a streetcar with race car speed. Oh, I forgot to mention that the car was also bulletproof, built for occasions like this. A street tank was what Mister called it. It was a great backup plan.

The four newly recruited guys trailed close behind us as we made our way down I-65 South towards Greenville, Alabama. These guys were Ex-Black Ops Marines that served under Todd Smith, AKA my Guardian Angel/Bodyguard. They were only four of eight that Todd and I hired for this new private unit called WIN, meaning When In Need. These guys were some real mercenaries that needed steady work. So I gave them a job under the supervision of Todd, who said that we couldn't put the old band back together.

When we arrived, the first person I noticed across the field was Bob Collins looking like Boss Hog from that hit television show in the early 80's called the Dukes of Hazzard. He was standing over there in his white suit, smoking on a damn cigar with his fat ass. My gut feeling told me that this muthafucka Bob wasn't coming out here for any peace talks or negotiations of peace. But, like my friend Kim would say, it's ok to look for the best in people and expect the worst is sure to come. The Collins had us outnumbered two-to-one. These muthafuckas were some hateful white supremacists, the bloodline of Neo-Nazism. They were some true savages sporting the damn Confederate flags all over their trucks like it was a sports team colors or some shit.

As Mister and I exited the car, Bob Collins shouted across the field. "KING, RELEASE MY BOY NOW!!!" Before I responded, I took a quick look around to make sure my guys were where they were supposed to be because this was a game of chess. Bob's next move needed to be his best move. "Ok! But what happened to the peace talk?" "THERE WON'T BE ANY PEACE TALKS

WITH YOU BLACK SONS-OF- BITCHES! THIS MUST END NOW!!!!!

Those were the words my crew was anticipating. So we all took cover behind our vehicles as Bob Collins, along with his two other sons and their crew of about twenty men, started firing their shotguns and assault rifles in the direction of my crew's two vehicles, just like I expected. No shots were being fired in the direction of the Monte Carlo because his son was still sitting in the back seat. That gave Mister and I a clear line of fire to pick some of their crew members off.

I couldn't help but think that Bob just knew he had outsmarted me and had my crew pinned down under heavy gunfire. He didn't account for the element of surprise, which came from behind them, as his crew members started being shot down one by one. Bob's crew began to panic, turned their attention away from us, and started firing their shots into the wooded area behind them, trying to shoot whoever it was that was picking them off from their backside. A handful of their guys tried to run but were quickly shot down by WIN.

At this point, the score was 14-0 in our favor, with the ball in our court. This war had finally come to an end. There were only two of Bob's crew breathing when the smoke cleared. One of the two happened to have been Mike Collins, Bob's oldest son. I stood over him, and before putting two shots into his head, I gave him a message to give to his father in hell. The message was, "save me a seat."

Bob Collins was an old-school mobster that preferred sitting around playing checkers. He never got around to learning how to play chess, which wiped out ninety-nine percent of his bloodline. I stayed three moves ahead of him in this war. I guess Bob never read the book The Art of War by Sun Tzu, either. Oh well.

"Hey Mister, get a message to Mrs. Collins telling her that her son Richie will be returned to her within the next twenty-four hours, but the other Collins wouldn't make it home for dinner tonight or ever again!" "So you gonna let the boy go, King?" "Yeah I am, Mister!" "Ok King, I understand that there are rules. but if we kill the kid, the Collins bloodline will be gone forever, and we won't have to worry about any revenge down the line."

"My Pops told me a long time ago, before they shipped me away, to respect the rules of the game. Because if you don't, the game won't respect you back. Rule #1 no killing of women or children in this thing of ours, the kids are the future." "Cool, say no more; I guess we will see him in about five to ten years." "Sooooo true, Mister." I said, laughing out loud. "So true."

Made in the USA
Columbia, SC
29 September 2024